CHARLES PORTIS'S
NORWOOD

"Portis does not patronize his comic-book reading troubador;
he marvels at him and touches his adventures along Route 67
with the magic of a fable."
—THE NEW YORK TIMES BOOK REVIEW

"One of the funniest books of the year...pure delight."
—THE NATIONAL OBSERVER

"Norwood is an absolute. He makes no comments and no
observations on America; instead he is America himself—the
true man of the modern West we have all seen in bus depots, an
innocent, guileless, perhaps infinitely wise tattoed philoso-
pher in blue jeans."
—THE WORCESTER TELEGRAM (MASS.)

"Portis is the funniest writer publishing today. He also has the
finest ear for dialogue."
—NEWSDAY

"Quiet and funny and very, very lovely...a thing to be remembered for a long, long time."
—THE CLEVELAND PLAIN DEALER

ALSO AVAILABLE IN VINTAGE CONTEMPORARIES

CHARLES PORTIS

NORWOOD

VINTAGE CONTEMPORARIES

VINTAGE BOOKS · A DIVISION OF RANDOM HOUSE · NEW YORK

First Vintage Books Edition, August 1985
Copyright © 1966 by Charles Portis
All rights reserved under International and Pan-American
Copyright Conventions. Published in the United States by
Random House, Inc., New York, and simultaneously in
Canada by Random House of Canada Limited, Toronto.
Originally published by Simon & Schuster, Inc., in 1966.
Library of Congress Cataloging in Publication Data
Portis, Charles.
Norwood.
(Vintage contemporaries)
Reprint. Originally published: New York:
Simon & Schuster, 1966.
Includes index.
I. Title.
PS3566.0663N6 1985   813'.54   85-7650.
ISBN 0-394-72931-5
Manufactured in the United States of America
Author photo copyright © 1985 by Jonathan Portis

FOR A.

NORWOOD HAD TO GET a hardship discharge when Mr. Pratt died because there wasn't anyone else at home to look after Vernell. Vernell was Norwood's sister. She was a heavy, sleepy girl with bad posture. She was old enough to look after herself and quite large enough, but in many ways she was a great big baby. Everybody out on the highway said, "What's going to happen to Vernell now?" Several people out there on the highway put this question to Brother Humphries and his reply was a thoughtful, "I don't know. I'm trying to work something out." He talked to a man in Texarkana who worked something out with the Red Cross man at Camp Pendleton and the Red Cross man in turn worked it out with the major who handled hardship discharges. Norwood had to see the major three times and talk to him about personal and embarrassing things. The major had a 105-millimeter ashtray on his desk. He was not an un-

7

kindly man and he expedited the matter as best he could. Norwood took his discharge, which he felt to be shameful, and boarded a bus in Oceanside that was bound for his home town of Ralph, Texas—with, of course, many intermediate stops. The big red-and-yellow cruiser had not gone far when Norwood remembered with a sinking heart that in all the confusion of checking out he had forgotten to go by Tent Camp 1 and pick up the seventy dollars that Joe William Reese owed him. This was a measure of his distress. It was not like Norwood to forget money. Joe William should have come by and paid him. *He* would have if *he* had owed the money. But no, that was not Joe William's way.

Thinking about it, on top of this discharge business, sent Norwood further into depression. He decided he would sit up straight all the way home and not look at the sights and not sleep and not push the Recline-o button and not lean back thirty or forty degrees the way he had planned. Nor would he talk to anyone. Except for short answers to direct and impersonal questions such as "Do you have the time?" or "What town is this?" But he did not sulk long. He slept for 335 miles, leaning back at the maximum Trailways angle, and when he awoke he struck up a conversation with a friendly young couple name of Remley. The Remleys had been picking asparagus in the Imperial

Valley and were now on their way home with their asparagus money. Traveling with them was their infant son Hershel. Hershel was a cheerful, bright-eyed little fellow. He was very well behaved and Norwood remarked on this.

Mrs. Remley patted Hershel on his tummy and said, "Say I'm not always this nice." Hershel grinned but said nothing.

"I believe the cat has got that boy's tongue," said Norwood.

"Say no he ain't," said Mrs. Remley. "Say I can talk aplenty when I want to, Mr. Man."

"Tell me what your name is," said Norwood. "What is your name?"

"Say Hershel. Say Hershel Remley is my name."

"How old are you, Hershel? Tell me how old you are."

"Say I'm two years old."

"Hold up this many fingers," said Norwood.

"He don't know about that," said Mrs. Remley. "But he can blow out a match."

Norwood talked to Mr. Remley about bird hunting. Mrs. Remley talked about her mother's people of near Sallisaw. Hershel made certain noises but said no words as such. Mrs. Remley was not bad looking. Norwood wondered why she had married Mr. Remley. One thing, though . . . he knew about bird dogs.

Norwood invited them to stop in Ralph and stay with him for a few days. He would borrow Clyde Rainey's dog and they could go quail hunting. Vernell was in bed sick with grief and beyond comfort when they arrived. She had not even been able to attend the funeral. Norwood put the Remleys in Mr. Pratt's old bedroom and he set up a cot for himself in the kitchen. Brother Humphries did not like the looks of the Remleys and he told Norwood as much. Or rather he told him that with Vernell here in bed and in the shape she was in and all, it might not be the best thing to be bringing in boomers like that off the bus. Norwood said they would only be there for a couple of days. Sometime during the night the Remleys decamped, taking with them a television set and a 16-gauge Ithaca Featherweight and two towels. No one could say how they got out of town with that gear, least of all the night marshal. The day marshal came by and looked at the place where the television set had been. He made notes.

Norwood and Vernell did not live right in Ralph but just the other side of Ralph. Mr. Pratt had always enjoyed living on the edge of places or between places, even when he had a choice. He was an alcoholic auto mechanic. Before his death they had moved a lot, back and forth along U.S. Highway 82 in the oil fields and cotton patches between Stamps, Arkansas, and Hooks, Texas. There was something Mr. Pratt dearly loved about that section of interstate concrete. They clung to its banks like river rats. Once, near Stamps, they lived in a house between a Tastee-Freez stand and a cinder-block holiness church. There had been a colorful poster on one side of the house that said ROYAL AMERICAN SHOWS OCT. 6-12 ARKANSAS LIVESTOCK EXPOSITION LITTLE ROCK. On the other side of the house somebody with a big brush and a can of Sherwin-Williams flat white had painted ACTS 2:38.

They later moved to a tin-roof house that was situated in a gas field under a spectacular flare that burned all the time. Big copper-green beetles the size of mice came from all over the Southland to see it and die in it. At night their little toasted corpses pankled down on the tin roof.

The Pratts did their washing and shaving on the front porch because that was where the pan was, and the mirror. You could see better out there. Little Vernel—when she *was* little—would stand out in the yard in her panties and wave a stick or a carburetor at all the transcontinental motorists. She may well have caught some of them going both ways—the salesmen in black Dodge business coupés with no back seats—

so frequently did the Pratts move from one side of the road to the other. Mr. Pratt did not prefer one side of U.S. 82 over the other.

When they moved to Ralph, Norwood quit school and went to work at the Nipper Independent Oil Co. Servicenter, and with his first money he built his mother a bathroom. He did all the carpentering and put in the fixtures himself. Most of the stuff was sec-ondhand—the water heater and the commode and the lumber—but he bought the bathtub new from Sears, and it *was* a delight. It was low and modern and sleek, with a built-in thing for the soap. There was a raised wave design on the bottom. Mrs. Pratt was well pleased and said so.

But she was gone these many years and now the old mechanic too, he who had shaken his head and wiped his hands and told at least a thousand people they were losing oil through the main bearing, had joined her. Norwood missed the funeral but Clyde Rainey had gone and he said it had all been very nice. More people came than reasonably could have been ex-pected. There were a good many flowers too. The funeral home had scrubbed Mr. Pratt down with Boraxo and Clyde said he had never seen him look-ing so clean and radiant.

Norwood picked up his old job at the Nipper station and Clyde was glad to have him back. Norwood was a good worker and was not known to be a thief. The station featured dishes and cheap gasoline. All credit cards were honored. The rest rooms were locked for the protection of the customers. Inside the station itself there was a tilted mirror along the back wall to deceive the eye and make the place look bigger. Outside, eye-catching banners and pennants and clever mobile signs fluttered and spun and wheeled over the pumps. On top of the station there was a giant billboard showing a great moon face with eyeglasses. It was a face beaming with good will. It was, of course, Nipper himself, the famous Houston oilman. A little cartoon body had been painted on beneath the face, with one hand holding a gas hose and the other extended to the public in a stage gesture, palm outward, something like Porky Pig when he is saying, "That's all, folks." Along the bottom of the sign there was a line of script, in quotation marks, indicating that it was a message direct from the Nipper pen. *"Thank you for riding with Nipper,"* it said. *"Won't you call again?"*

Vernell cried and moped around the house for almost two months. Brother Humphries' wife and the other ladies of the church were good about bringing food over. They brought fried chicken and potato salad and coconut cakes and macaroni and cheese and baked sweet potatoes with marshmallows melted on top. The Home Demonstration agent came by and gave Vernell some housekeeping tips and some printed matter. When the woman left, Vernell went back to bed and forgot all the tips. But in time she came around. One morning she got up and washed her face and cooked Norwood's breakfast. She was still a little sickly though and the doctor told Norwood not to let her work too hard. He continued to do most of the cooking and housekeeping, and he stayed close and busied himself with little personal projects.

Sometimes he sat on the back steps wearing a black hat with a Fort Worth crease and played his guitar—just three or four chords really—and sang "Always Late—With Your Kisses," with his voice breaking like Lefty Frizzell, and "China Doll" like Slim Whitman, whose upper range is hard to match. The guitar wasn't much. It was a cheap West German model with nylon strings he had bought at the PX. He also put in a lot of time on his car. He had bought a 1947 Fleetline Chevrolet with dirt dobber nests in the heater and radio for fifty dollars. He put in some rings and ground the valves and got it in fair running shape. He loosened the tappets and put up with the noise so as to keep Vernell—who *would* race a motor—from burning the valves. She burned a connecting rod instead.

He made home improvements too. He ripped off the imitation brick siding on the house—Mr. Pratt had called it nigger brick—and slapped two coats of white paint on the walls in three days. He cleaned up the front yard and hauled off all the truck differentials and engine blocks and disembodied fenders, and took down the "I Do Not Loan Tools" sign from the persimmon tree. He thinned out the weeds in the big ditch in front of the house with a weed sling and gave the mosquitoes down there fits with twenty gallons of used motor oil. He had two loads of pea gravel dumped and spread over the driveway and he whitewashed some big rocks and laid them out for borders. There was some lime left over so he soaked some more rocks and laid out a globe-eagle-and-anchor emblem on the ditch slope facing the highway. He put his serial number under it.

One night he came home from work and said, "I'm tard of working at that station, Vernell."

"What's wrong, bubba?"

"Every time you grease a truck stuff falls in your eyes and your hair and down your back. You got it pretty easy yourself. You know that?"

"Why don't you get a hat?"

"I got plenty of hats, Vernell. I don't need any more hats. If all I needed was another hat I would be well off."

"What do you want to do?"

"I want to get on the *Louisiana Hayride.*"

"Well, why don't you go over there and get on it, then?"

"You can't just go over there and get on it. They have to know something about you. You have to audition. They don't just let anybody on it that wants to. I guess you thought people just showed up at KWKH and said I want to be on the *Hayride.*"

"You're as good as some of 'em I've heard on it."

"I know I'm *good* enough to be on it. That's not it."

"Well look, let me have a half a dollar so I can go to the show with Lorene."

"Let you have a half a dollar?"

"I'm going to the show with Lorene."

"I wish I had somebody around to give me half a dollars. I have to work for mine. They don't give me anything down there at the station. I have to work for every dime and then pay taxes on that. I never even see that tax money."

"I know, you told me about that."

"You don't act like it. I'll tell you something else. Maybe I would have some money if people paid me what they owed me. Joe William Reese owes me seventy dollars and has never paid me to this day."

"You told me about that."

"He'll never pay me that money."

"Maybe he will sometime."

"Naw he won't."

"He might. You ought to write him or call him. He might of forgot it his own self."

"You don't even know him, Vernell. If you knew him you wouldn't say that."

After Vernell had gone to the show Norwood went back to the station and used the phone. He called the Reese residence in Old Carthage, Arkansas. An old woman answered who talked very fast. She said Joe William had come, shed his uniform, and gone, and was now believed to be in New York City.

"What is he doing up there?"

"Lord, I don't know. Don't ask me."

"When will he be back?"

"He didn't say. We don't look for him any time soon. I don't anyway. Old Carthage is too little for Joe William. Who is this?"

"This is Norwood Pratt over in Ralph, Texas. I wanted to talk to him about some money he owes me."

"Who? Joe William?"

"Yes ma'am."

"What was your name?"

"Pratt. Norwood Pratt."

"I don't believe we know any Pratts in Texas. There's a J. B. Pratt here that sweeps out the court-house. He used to come around and sharpen scissors. I don't know when I've seen that old man. He always did good work."

"Joe William and me was in the arm service to-gether."

"Say you were?"

"Yes ma'am."

"Well, I don't know what to tell you. I'm his grand-mother. But I'm a Whichcoat. That is I married a Whichcoat. My daughter was a Whichcoat before she married Joe William's father. The Reeses all came in here from Tennessee after the war. The sawmill was here then, and the compress too. Well, one compress is still here for that matter, but they tore the big one down, oh Lord, *years* ago. My maiden name is Finch. You've probably heard of old Judge Finch. He was on the Fourth Circuit here for so long? All the papers have written him up.'"

"Have you got Joe William's address there?"

"I'll have to ask Daughter about that."

Norwood wrote Joe William a card at the New York address and watched the mail with anxiety for three weeks. It was worse than waiting on something from Sears. Nothing came. He wrote another one and put an extra stamp on it this time. There was no answer. Clyde Rainey said, "What's bothering you, Norwood?"

"Nothing."

"You don't seem to have your mind on your business."

"I'm all right."

"Are you feeling all right?"

"I'm fine, Clyde. If there was anything wrong with me I would go to the doctor."

"You don't look right to me."

One warm summer evening, shortly after the Ralph B&PW Club had given up on trying to teach Vernell how to type, Norwood was out in the yard cutting the grass with a push mower he had borrowed from the station. He took his shirt off and then put it on again. The mosquitoes were fierce. Vernell was sitting on the front porch with a dishpan in her lap, shelling peas. She said, "I wonder if Mama and Daddy can look down from heaven tonight and see how nice the yard looks." Norwood stopping mowing. "I don't know, Vernell. Did you go down and talk to that woman at the hotel today like I told you to?"

"Well, I had some things to do. I'll go one day next week."

"Naw you won't. You'll go the first thing in the morning."

She cried and took some aspirins and went to bed, but Norwood hauled her out the next morning and made her dress and shave and he told her that she was going to be working at the New Ralph Hotel Coffee Shop that very day or he would know the reason why.

"I don't feel good, bubba," she pleaded. "I don't know how to do it. I'm liable to get the orders wrong."

"I got you this job and you're going down there. Just get that through your head."

"What if I get the orders wrong?"

"Well, don't get 'em wrong. Get 'em right."

"I don't think I can do it."

"Yes, you can."

"I can't."

"Look, all you do is write on these tickets what they want and take it back to the cook's window. Anybody can do that. Listen. A man will come in and you will give him a glass of water and a menu. Then he will study it and decide what he wants. All right. If he wants number two, you put number two on this side of the ticket and then the price over here. He might want some tea too. All right, put a big T under the number two and the price of the tea over there under the number two price. Then when he's through you add up all the prices and put on the tax and that's his bill. You ask him if there will be anything else and then give him his bill."

"I know all that."

"You are too afraid of people, Vernell. That's your trouble."

The job worked out too well. Money and position went to Vernell's head. She stopped crying. Her health and posture improved. She even became something of a flirt. She grew daily more confident and assertive and at home she would drop the names of prominent Lions and Kiwanians. Norwood listened in cold silence as she brought home choice downtown gossip and made familiar references to undertakers and lawyers and Ford dealers. Norwood had nothing to counter with. No one you could quote traded at the Nipper station. The customers were local Negroes and high school kids, and out-of-state felons in flight from prosecution and other economy-minded transients, most of whom carried their own strange motor oil in their back seats, oil that was stranger and cheaper than anything even in the Nipper inventory. Some weeks, with her tips, Vernell made more money than Norwood. It was a terrible state of affairs and Norwood would not have believed that things were to become worse almost overnight.

Then with absolutely no warning Vernell married a disabled veteran named Bill Bird and brought him home to live in the little house on the highway. Bill Bird was an older man. He had drifted into Ralph for no very clear reason after being discharged from the VA hospital in Dallas. He took a room at the New Ralph Hotel, monthly rate, and passed his time in the coffee shop, at the corner table under the fan, reading *Pageant* and *Grit* and pondering the graphs in *U.S. News & World Report*. Vernell took to Bill Bird at once. She liked his quiet, thoughtful air and his scholarship. She kept his cup filled with coffee and during lulls she would sit at his table and enjoy him. Bill Bird was at the same time attentive to Vernell in many little ways.

One afternoon she said, "I declare, Bill, you just read all the time. It must make your eyes hurt."

Bill Bird shook himself out of a hypnotic reading trance and put his paper down and rose to offer her a chair. "Sit down, Vernell. Relax for a minute. You're working too hard."

"Well, I will for just a minute."

Bill Bird tapped the newspaper with his pipe. "I was reading an interesting little piece there in the *Grit*. A retired high school band director in Fort Lauderdale, Florida, has taught his fox terrier to play "Springtime in the Rockies" on the mouth harp. He holds it on with a little wire collar device. Like this."

"Well, I'll be," said Vernell. "A dog playing songs. I'd like to see that. I bet that's cute."

"That wasn't what I meant," said Bill Bird. "I mean I suppose it *is* cute, but it's more than that. It goes to show that animals are a lot smarter than people think. I honestly believe that one day we may be able to talk to them. By that I mean *communicate* in some fashion. There's a lot of interesting research going on in that field."

"What else can he sing, that dog?"

"Well, it doesn't say. It just says he is limited to a few simple melodies because of his small lungs. Now he doesn't *sing*, Vernell. He *plays* these songs on a mouth organ. A harmonica. His name is Tommy."

"I'd like to hear that scamp play. They ought to put him on television sometime."

Bill Bird hummed the opening of "Springtime in the Rockies" and thought about it for a minute. "That's not exactly a simple tune, you know. I think it represents a pretty amazing range for a dog."

"You must know something about every subject in the world, Bill. Somebody could sit here and write a book just listening to you."

"Oh I don't know about that, Vernell. I will admit this: I have always been curious about things. The world about me. Like most of your scientists

I am interested in the *why* of things, and not just the *what*. Sometimes I think I might have been happier if I didn't have such a searching mind."

"You couldn't be any other way. You know that."

"Some people go through their entire lives and are are completely satisfied with the *what*. They don't ask questions."

"They don't know any better."

"They are content to go along in the old patterns, the same old ruts, never realizing how much richer and fuller their lives could be."

"That's all they know."

"How much does your man on the street know of psychology?"

"Nothing. They don't know anything."

"How many of them can even vote intelligently? I was reading in *Parade* the other day that more people can identify Dick Tracy than the Vice President."

"People ought to read more. And not just the funnies either."

Norwood knew Bill Bird on sight and he had heard Vernell speak of him often enough but he had no idea anything was up. And now here he was, this middle-aged stranger, in Norwood's home, at his breakfast table, in his bathroom. It was not clear how or where or even in what war Bill Bird had fallen. Sometimes he spoke of Panama. There seemed to be nothing much wrong with him, apart from irregularity and low metabolism. He had all his limbs, his appetite was good.

Bill Bird received a lot of official brown mail, and, no doubt, a regular check, but he did not offer to pay anything toward the general household expenses. After meals he would excuse himself and go to the bedroom and close the door. He kept a little duffel bag in there filled with supplementary treats for his own exclusive use—Vienna sausages, olives, chocolate chip cookies. He had no problem adjusting from hotel life to home life. He bumped around the house, sockless, in some tan, army-looking dress shoes and an old corduroy VA robe. He was in and out of the bathroom with his magazines. He made an hourly circuit through the kitchen to look in the stove and the refrigerator and all the cabinets and the breadbox and indeed into everything that had a door.

Norwood did not like the sound of Bill Bird's voice. Bill Bird was originally from some place in Michigan and Norwood found his brisk Yankee vowels offensive. They argued about the bathroom. Bill Bird had made himself a little home in that bathroom. He used all the hot water. He filled up the cabinet with dozens of little bottles with typing on them, crowding Norwood's shaving gear out and onto the windowsill. He

used Norwood's blades. He left hairs stuck around
in the soap—short, gray, unmistakable Bill Bird hairs.
Norwood had built the bathroom, it was his, and the
thought of Bill Bird's buttocks sliding around on the
bottom of the modern Sears tub was disagreeable.
They argued about the Marine Corps. Bill Bird said
it was vastly overrated. He cited personal experiences
and magazine articles. For all the Marines' talk of the
Halls of Montezuma, he said, there had actually been
only a handful of Marines at the siege of Chapultepec.
Regular army troops, as usual, had won the day there.

Norwood said he had been told by people who
knew that certain army units in Korea in 1950 had
abandoned their weapons and equipment and even
their wounded while under Chinese attack. Many
of the wounded had been rescued by Marines. Bill
Bird said he knew this to be untrue. He also informed
Norwood that it was a Federal offense to strike a disabled veteran, not to say ruinous damage-wise in the
courts. They argued too about Norwood's plan to
leave his job at the Nipper station and strike out
blindly for Shreveport and a musical career on the
Louisiana Hayride, the celebrated Country and Western show presented Saturday nights on KWKH, a
50,000-watt clear channel station serving the Ark-
LaTex. It was foolish, Bill Bird said, to leave a job before you were sure you had another job. Vernell said

that made plenty of sense to her. Bill Bird said that if
you had a job you could always get a job. Vernell con-
curred. He went on to say that it was hard to get a
job if you did not already have a job. "Bill is right
about that," said Vernell. They argued about the
seventy-dollar debt and ways and means of collecting
it. Bill Bird said the best approach would be to pay
some lawyer ten or fifteen dollars to write that fellow
a scare letter. "Then I would be out eighty-five dollars," said Norwood. Well, said Bill Bird, he, for one,
was tired of hearing about that confounded seventy
dollars.

The compactness of the Pratt house was such that
three-way conversations could be and very often were
carried on from three different rooms, with none of
the parties visible to the others. "You beat anything
I ever saw, bubba," said Vernell, who was in the bedroom ironing on this night. "We're both of us making
good money now and we got the house fixed up and
you've got your car and Bill's here and you just want
to throw it all to one side and take off for Shreveport.
You don't even know anybody in Shreveport."

Norwood was sitting at the kitchen table eating a
warmed-over supper. He'd been late getting home
from the station and they had not waited. He kept his
hat on while he ate, his pale green Nipper hat with
the black bill. It was a model the Miami Police De-

partment had used in 1934. He held his left thumb in a glass of ice water. The thumb, sticky with shaving cream, was swelling and throbbing and purpling. He had fixed flats that day for three big state gravel trucks, one after the other, and when he was breaking down one of the wheels a locking ring had snapped back on his thumb.

"Well, when you get in Shreveport and run out of money," came the Michigan voice of Bill Bird, through a cloud of bathroom steam, "Vernell and I will not be able to send you any."

Norwood speared a sausage patty with his fork and gave it a hard flip through the bathroom doorway.

"Hey!" said Bill Bird. "All right now!" He emerged from the steam in some green VA convalescent pants that were cinched up with a drawstring. Except for his tan shoes, that was all he had on. He was holding the sausage on his open palm, level, like a compass, and he was studying it. "Did you throw this, Norwood?"

"What is it, Bill?"

"You know what it is. It's a sausage."

"I wondered what that was," said Norwood. "I saw a arm come in the back door there and chunk something acrost the room. I thought maybe there was a note on it."

Bill Bird called into the bedroom. "Vernell, come in here a minute. I want you. Norwood's throwing food."

Vernell came in and looked at Bill Bird's naked torso. "Goodness, Bill, put on some clothes. Norwood's trying to eat his supper."

"Look at this," said Bill Bird.

"That's a sausage," she said.

"I know what it is. He threw it at me in the bathroom."

"What for? What would he want to throw a sausage for?"

"I don't know, Vernell. It's beyond me. I *do* know you could very easily put someone's eye out like that."

She gave a little laugh. "I don't think you could put anybody's eye out with a sausage." Then she saw from Bill Bird's face that this was not the ticket. She turned to Norwood. "What made you want to do it, bubba?"

Norwood went on eating. "You two would drive anybody crazy," he said. "Going on all night about a sausage."

"It's something you would expect out of a child," said Bill Bird. "You know I've tried to get along with him, Vernell, but you can't treat him like a responsible adult. He should be made to apologize for this. *Now* would be the time for it."

"Bubba, tell Bill you're sorry. Come on now. It won't hurt you."

"I don't know why I ought to apologize if some stranger comes along and throws a sausage in the house at *him*. All I saw was his sleeve, Bill. I couldn't tell what color it was, it happened so fast."

"I'll tell you what's going to become of your brother, Vernell," said Bill Bird. "He's going to wind up in the penitentiary. They have some people there who will set him straight on a few things. You can count on that. I read an article the other day about the seven danger signs of criminal tendencies in the young. I've marked it in there for you to read. I think you will be a little disturbed, you should be, to learn that your own brother has the same personality profile as Alvin Karpis."

"Bubba was just playing with you, Bill."

"I'll say this: Unless his attitude undergoes a great change he will be in the pen within five years, just as sure as we're standing here. Now. We'll consider this incident closed."

Norwood made himself two biscuit and Br'er Rabbit Syrup sandwiches and went out on the front porch to eat them and wait on the bath water to get hot. Down the highway beyond the Nipper station

the lights of the skating rink made a dull yellow
glow. Insect bulbs of low wattage. The music came
and went in heavy waves. It was a record of a boogie-
woogie organist playing "Under the Double Eagle."
Norwood threw one of the biscuit sandwiches out to
a red dog that was traveling through town, going
east, possibly to Texarkana, and watched him eat it
in one gulp. Then he went out and started the Fleetline and listened for a minute to the clatter of the
burnt rod and the loose tappets—it sounded like a
two-cylinder John Deere tractor—and drove down to
the skating rink. Sometimes, after the first session,
you could pick up a country girl there looking for a
ride home.

It was a clear warm Friday night and there was a
big crowd. The tent flaps were rolled up all the way
around. Some of the bolder girls were wearing short
pleated skirts that bounced. The boys were skating
fast, working hard at it, as though they were deliver-
ing important telegrams. Out front some Future
Farmers of America were horsing around beside a
billet truck, playing keep-away with a softball. The
boy they were keeping it away from was smoking a
cigarette and was also wearing an FFA jacket. "Here,
you want it? I'm really gonna let you have it this
time." The boy would never learn. They were keeping it away from him because he looked like a ba-

boon. Norwood wandered around to the back of the tent and stood by himself leaning against a big pecan tree and watching the skaters through the chicken wire. He was there only a minute or two, checking out the girls, when he heard someone cracking nuts on the other side of the tree.

He peered around for a look. A very thin and yet very broad man was standing there expertly cracking pecans in his hands and getting the meats out whole. He was as flat and wide as a gingerbread man. He was wearing a smooth brown saddle-stitched sport jacket and some blue slacks with hard creases and a pearl-gray cattleman's hat. He grinned and dusted the hulls from his huge flat hands and extended one to Norwood.

"Hello there, Norwood."

Norwood shook his hand. "I thought I heard somebody back there. Do you know me?"

"Well, I feel like I do. I see your name stitched there over your pocket. Of course you might have someone's else's shirt on. In that case your name might very well be Earl or Dub for all I know."

"Naw, it's my shirt all right."

"My name is Fring. I'm glad to know you, Norwood. Tell me, is everyone at home well?"

"Just getting along fine. How about your folks?"

"They're all dead except for me and my brother

Tilmon. I'm fine and he's doing very well, considering his age. Here, take this home and read it when you get a minute." He handed Norwood a pamphlet. It said, *A non-cancellable guaranteed renewable for life hospitilization policy, underwritten by one of the Mid-South's most reliable insurance firms. No age limit. PAYS up to $5,000.00 for sickness or accident. PAYS up to $400.00 for surgery. PAYS prescription benefits. PAYS home nurse benefits. PAYS iron lung fees. PAYS* . . . "You don't have to read it now. Take it home and study it later. Compare it with your present program, in light of your current insurance needs. Talk it over with those at home. That little policy just sells itself."

Norwood put it in his pocket. "A insurance man."

"Well, among other things, yes. My brother Tilmon and I have a good many business interests. I'm also in mobile homes and coin-operated machines. I am a licensed private investigator in three states. We have a debt collection agency in Texarkana. I know you've heard of our car lots over there. Grady Fring?"

"You're not Grady Fring the Kredit King?"

"I am indeed."

"No reasonable offer refused."

"The very same."

"You can't convince Grady your credit is bad."

"Right again."

33

Norwood laughed. "Well, this *is* something. I've seen your signs and heard your things on the radio a lot. *Grady has gone crazy* and all that."

"I would certainly be disappointed if you hadn't heard them," said Grady. "If I told you what our advertising budget was last year, you wouldn't believe it. That's where you've got to put your money if you want to move the goods. You know what I believe in?"

"What?"

"Volume."

"What?"

"Volume. Volume. I don't care what I make off anything—six dollars, a quarter, a dime—as long as I can move it. Sell it! Move it! Give it away! But just clear it on out of the way and bring something else in, and then we'll sell it too. Yessir, I do believe in volume. Why aren't you out there skating with all those pretty girls?"

"I'm not too good a skater."

"Do you come out here much?"

"Some. Every now and then."

"I'll bet you know all those girls out there."

"I know some of 'em."

"This is my first visit," said Grady, "to this particular roller drome. I get around a good deal at night, you see. I am also connected with a New Orleans tal-

34

ent agency and that part of my work takes me around to many . . . highway institutions. What our agency does—it's fully licensed—is seek out and recruit lovely young girls over the Mid-South. Girls seeking a career in show business. Girls who want to leave home. You may not realize it but we have some of the sweetest little girls in the country right around in these parts."

"We sure do."

"I'd put them up against girls from anywhere."

"That Cresswell girl is a good skater," said Norwood. "She's about the best one around here. That one there with the lights on her skates."

"Yes, I've had my eye on her. She's a dandy. And sweet too. Do you know her folks? What does her daddy do?"

"I don't know what he does. Her mama works down at the Washateria."

"How old is she?"

"About fifty-six."

"No, I mean the girl."

"Oh. She's about seventeen. I think she gets out of high school this year."

"I'd rather not fool with them if they're under nineteen or twenty. You will understand, Norwood, I am not necessarily looking for skating skills. What about you, do you live here in town?"

"Yeah. I live down there just the other side of that Nipper station."

"Old Nipper! I was looking at your uniform when you first came up. He's an old friend of mine, you know, Nipper is. I used to do some investigating for him down in Houston. I was practicing a little law then too. What a man! Money? Norwood, he's richer than the fabled Croesus. Have you ever met him?"

"I never did. I seen his plane a few times. He used to fly over town dropping out copies of the Constitution."

"Well, he's quite a man. I was on his education committee for three years and I was a judge in the Nipper Junior High Essay Contests that were so big. I was one of the judges. Perhaps you sent one in yourself?"

"What?"

"The Nipper Essay Contest. For junior high kids."

"I didn't hear anything about it."

"You should have got in on that, Norwood. Everybody got a little prize of some kind. And the winners, we gave them some wonderful scholarships. Their theme was 'Communism in the National Council of Churches.' They laid it right on the line. Wrote their hearts out. I was proud to be a part of it."

"Do you still work for Nipper?"

"No, not any more. We had a falling out, I'm sorry to say. I traded him some rent houses for a registered bull and he got mad about it. Subsequently I left Houston."

"Did you beat him on the trade?"

"Yes, I confess that I did. I took him like Stonewall Jackson took Nathaniel P. Banks in the Valley of the Shenandoah. That is to say, decisively."

"He didn't like that."

"He wasn't used to it."

Norwood looked at his watch. "Well, I got to get on back to the house and take a bath. My thumb's hurting."

Grady touched his arm. "Wait a minute. I'd like to talk to you about something. I *might* be able to put you next to something. Have you got a couple of minutes?"

"Yeah, I guess so."

"I tell you what we *could* do. We *could* go over to my car and have a drink and talk about it there."

"All right."

It was a big new Buick Invicta with red leather upholstery. Grady brought out a bottle of Old Forester from under the seat. There was some crushed ice in a milk shake carton. Norwood held the paper cups and Grady poured.

"This is a nice car," said Norwood.

"Yes, I'm doing right well," said Grady. "How many tubes do you think that radio has?"

"I don't know. It looks like a good one."

"Twenty-four. There's not another one like it in this part of the country. Listen to that tone. It's like FM."

Norwood listened. "That tone *is* good."

"What happened to your thumb?"

"Nothing. I mashed it."

"You better put something on it when you get home."

"I already did."

"Unguentine is good for something like that."

"I put some shaving cream on it."

"Unguentine is a lot better. It has special healing ingredients that shaving cream doesn't have. It goes to work on that soreness."

"Was that what you wanted to tell me?"

"No," said Grady, and he took off his hat and arranged himself sideways on the seat in the attitude of a man getting down to business. "No, it's something else. You're a big strong boy, Norwood. I've got a place for you, I think. Here's the deal: We buy these bad debts from stores and filling stations at twelve cents on the dollar. Then we go out and collect what we can. A top-notch, hustling, aggressive agent can make good on forty per cent of that paper. He can make those profligate bastards cough up. And anybody, with my training, can make good on twenty-five per cent of it. I'll train you and buy you a suit and some Florsheim shoes and furnish you with one of my late model demonstrator cars and we split halves on everything above the line. Everything above my twelve per cent investment. What do you think?"

"I don't think I would be much good at that."

"You're not interested in making money."

"Naw, I didn't say that. I said I didn't think I would be much good at it. I got a debt of my own I can't collect. Another thing is, I don't have much education. For that kind of job. Wearing a suit."

"Education requirements are minimal. Let me be the judge of that."

"Well, naw, I don't think so."

"Hmmm," said Grady, and he poured some more of the Forester. "Tell me this, how would you like a trip to California?"

"I been to California."

"That doesn't mean you can't go again."

"It's too far."

"How about a trip to Chicago? . . . New York? . . . Atlanta?"

"New York?"

39

"That's right, New York City. A wonderful trip, all expenses paid. Plus—and get this—fifty dollars clear for you, found money, right off the top."

"This is not some kind of contest."

"No, no, this is a straightforward job offer. Are you a good driver?"

"Yeah."

"Good enough. You see, Tilmon and I ship off some of our surplus cars, our good ones, to other parts of the country, where we can get a better price for them. It's the drivers who have all the fun. Speeding across the country in a late model car, seeing all the sights."

"I would take one to New York."

"That's it."

"How long would it take?"

"You'll be back in a week after a wonderful paid-for trip. Many of your friends will envy—"

"How would I get back?"

"You drive back. That's part of the deal. You take one up and bring one back."

"I don't get that."

"What is it you don't get?"

"Well, if I take one up and bring another one back, you're right back where you started. I don't see how that would put you ahead much."

"That's because you don't understand the market.

Some cars are worth more up there and some are worth more down here because of freight costs and other variables. Take a Mercedes now, it will cost you a good two hundred dollars more down here. It all has to do with the market. You won't be dead-heading back, don't worry about that."

"I hope these are not stolen cars."

Grady looked at Norwood for a long moment. "I don't know whether you meant that seriously or not. We are legitimate businessmen, Norwood. We are in the public eye. We hold a position of trust in the community. We could hardly afford to jeopardize that position by playing around with hot cars. I think you spoke before you thought. No, we welcome legal scrutiny of all our affairs at all times."

"I don't want to get in any trouble."

"Naturally not. One way to avoid it would be not to repeat your highly actionable remark about hot cars."

"I *do* need to see somebody in New York."

Grady put on his glasses and consulted a billfold calendar by the light of his twenty-four-tube radio. "Hmmm. How does a next Sunday morning departure sound to you?"

"That's pretty quick."

Grady shrugged.

"I don't know," said Norwood. "I'd have to think

41

about it. I'd have to talk to my sister about it."

"By all means, talk to your sister. Discuss it with her. What is her name?"

"Vernell."

"What a lovely name," said Grady. He reached in the back seat and fumbled around in a big pasteboard box and brought forth a styrene comb and brush set and a little bottle of perfume with a blue bow on it. "Give this to Vernell with my warmest regards." He nodded toward the back seat. "We had a lot of honorable mention prizes left over in the last Nipper contest."

"This is mighty nice of you."

Grady waved it off. "It's nothing. Now. My phone number's on this card. Feel free to call me at any time, collect. I would appreciate it if you called on this matter by Thursday noon."

The ice in the milk shake carton was now soupy but they had another short drink anyway. When Norwood opened the door to leave, Grady had an afterthought. "Wait a minute," he said. "Let me see your watch." Norwood showed it to him. Grady studied it critically through the reading part of his glasses, under the radio light. He tapped the crystal with a long, dense, yellow fingernail. "With all respect to you, that's a piece of junk." Then he slipped his own watch off, a flat shiny one with a black face and gold pips instead of numbers, and gave it to Norwood. "I don't want you to go home tonight till you have a good timepiece on your wrist. You can just put that other one away in your drawer somewhere. Sell it to a nigger if you can. . . . No, don't say a word. I want you to have it. I get these at well below cost."

"This is mighty nice of you, Mr. Fring."

"Mr. Fring nothing. Call me Grady."

Norwood drove home and thought about how he would put it to Clyde about taking off from the station. Clyde would ask five hundred questions. Vernell and Bill Bird would be a problem too. They would gnaw on it for days like two puppies with a rubber bone. Norwood had a long reflective bath. He put some more shaving cream on his thumb. While he was combing his hair he took up an oblique pose in front of the mirror and gave himself a lazy smile, like some smirking C & W star coming up out of the lower right-hand corner of an 8 by 10 glossy.

He played some records for a while in his sleeping porch bedroom and imagined himself having a smoke backstage with Lefty Frizzell: *Hey Norwood, you got a light?* His green pinstripe Nipper trousers were hanging on the back of a chair, with Grady's insurance tract sticking up out of a hip pocket. Norwood got up from bed in his shorts and took the tract into the front bedroom. He turned on the light, giving the sleeping Bill Birds quite a start.

"Get out of here," said Bill Bird.

"What is it, bubba? What do you want?"

"I found the note that was on that sausage, Bill. You didn't look hard enough."

"Turn that light off and get out."

"What does it say, bubba?"

"It says, 'Dear Bill Bird. If you know what's good for you you'll stop talking about things you don't know anything about. Yours truly, the Commandant of the Marine Corps.'"

"That's very funny. Now get out. I'm not going to tell you again."

"We're trying to sleep, bubba. Bill needs his rest."

VERNELL and Bill Bird did
not approve of the New York trip. "You don't even
know anybody in New York," said Vernell. Norwood
was shining his thirty-eight-dollar stovepipe boots.
They were coal-black 14-inchers with steel shanks
and low walking heels. Red butterflies were inset on
the insteps. He was putting a mirror gloss on the toes
with lighter fluid and a nylon stocking.

"You can't reason with him, Vernell," said Bill
Bird. "It's like talking to a child. I think we have
made our position clear. Even to him. I hope so. I
hope he's not planning on wiring us for money when
he gets up there stranded."

Norwood ignored him. "Vernell, don't be driving
my car much while I'm gone. If you have to use it
take it easy. That bad rod is liable to go at any time.
I'm afraid it's already scored the crankshaft. I'll have

to turn that goose when I get back. . . . I don't want *him* driving it at all."

Vernell thought this was unfair. "Bill can drive a car all right."

"Naw he can't."

"He can too. He's just used to an automatic transmission."

"Uh huh."

"Bill can drive as good as I can."

"Well, you can't drive either. The only thing is, you're my sister. I might as well turn my car over to a rabbit."

"You'd have to get special extensions for the pedals," said Bill Bird.

"Now I mean it, Vernell," said Norwood. "I don't want to come back here and have somebody tell me they seen Bill Bird driving around town in that car. Let him walk. It'll do him good."

Norwood rode to Texarkana early Sunday morning in the rain with a boy in a butane truck who had a date over there for church. He wore his black hat, the brim curled up in front to defy wind resistance, and his stovepipe boots. One trouser leg was tucked in and the other hung free, after the fashion. The boots were glorious. He had his sunglasses on too, and his heavy Western belt buckle, which portrayed a branding scene in silver relief.

Except for those stylish items, he was not really dressed up. There was a job to be done and a long drive ahead. His good slacks and his tight tailored shirt, with curved arrow pockets and pearl snaps, were packed away in a canvas AWOL bag. He was dressed for the trip in a starchy, freshly ironed Nipper uniform. At the last minute he decided to take along the West Germany guitar. It was zipped up in a soft clear plastic case.

The Kredit King was waiting in his Buick in front of the Texarkana post office as per the arrangement. He was deep in conversation with a man who was leaning on his window. The man was holding a cardboard bucket with GRADY'S BAIT RANCH printed on it. Norwood put his gear in the back seat and got in the front. The man outside straightened up to leave and Grady shook his hand through the window. "There's plenty of corn meal in there. They don't eat much. All you want to do is sprinkle a little water in there every two or three days." When the man left, Norwood said, "Who was that?"

"I don't know," said Grady. "Some fellow passing through town. He wanted to know if there were any opportunities here for a taxidermist. I'll talk to anybody. Talk to a *nigger* and you might learn something. I sold him four hundred worms." He looked at his watch. "You're right on the money, Norwood. I

47

like a man who does what he says he'll do."

"I got me a good watch."

"You have for a fact. . . . Here, let me get a look at you. That's all right. You look like the Durango Kid, perhaps better known as Charles Starrett. What's the guitar for?"

"It's mine, I thought I'd take it with me."

"You didn't tell me you were a musician."

"I fool around with it a little, that's all."

"You should have said something about it. I have a few contacts in the music game."

"You do?"

"Well, I know some of those boys. I have some music machines down around Bossier City."

"Do you know anybody on the *Louisiana Hayride?*"

"I know everybody on the *Louisiana Hayride.*"

"That's what I'd like to get a shot at."

"I expect I could pick up the phone and do you some good. We'll talk about that another day. Right now we'd best get to the business at hand. I know you're anxious to get rolling."

Grady unfolded a map of New York City and laid it out on the steering wheel. The delivery point, a garage in Brooklyn, was marked with a circle. Grady explained about the route. It was very complicated. He went over it again, then once more. Norwood lied and said he thought he had it. Grady gave him the map and a stiff fiber envelope holding titles and pink slips and two sets of keys and a Gulf credit card in the name of Tilmon Fring and twenty-five dollars expense money.

Norwood said, "I guess I'll get some more in New York then."

"Some more what?"

"Well. I don't know. Some more money."

"Wasn't that credit card in there?"

"Yeah, there's a credit card here. But I was wondering if this was enough money." He held up the five fives.

Grady was baffled and hurt. "That's the usual. I thought it would be ample. I've never had this come up before. This is embarrassing. You have your credit card. Figure a six-day trip at the very outside, that's more than four dollars a day for your meals and the little contingencies of the road. These warm nights you can pull over and catnap right there in the car if you get tired. Most of the drivers drive straight through. Arnold has a comfortable cot in his garage—"

"When do I get the fifty dollars?"

"When you get back. Cash on delivery."

"I couldn't get it now?"

"Why no. You're not even bonded, Norwood."

"What does that mean?"

"That means you get your money when you get back."

"I'd like to have some of it now."

Grady showed signs of distress. He took a kitchen match from his pocket, one with garlands of blue lint on it, and burrowed earnestly in one ear with it. When he was through he examined the match and buzzed down the automatic window a couple of inches and tossed it out. He brought his billfold from his inside coat pocket. "Here's what I'll do, Norwood. I've never done this before. I'll give you another ten toward expenses. We'll write that off. That's expenses. Then—I'll give you an advance of twenty-five. That's off your fifty. Now I'll hold the balance here—*on my person*—and then, see, you'll have that much more when you get back. To buy things that you need and want. Go off to New York with a lot of money and you'll *spend* a lot of money. I've seen it happen too often. . . . You know, some people would be willing to pay *us* for an opportunity like this."

Norwood counted the money and folded it into a hard square and stuck it in his watch pocket.

"Okay?" said Grady.

"Okay."

"You won't have to sign a voucher on that advance. And you needn't bother to make an exact accounting on the expense money. We're informal. We like to give our agents a free hand. So far as it's consistent with good business practice." He started the car and turned to Norwood with a grin. "I have a surprise waiting for you."

They drove half a mile or so through the Arkansas side of town and pulled into an alley full of puddles, behind an ice plant. As it turned out there were two surprises. The first was that there were two cars to be delivered, not one. There they were, bumper to bumper, a big 98 Oldsmobile in front and a Pontiac Catalina behind, gleaming and smelling pleasantly of new paint. "We always give them a coat of Duco," said Grady. "It's a small enough investment and it can add two hundred dollars to a car's value. That Olds is like new. Twelve thousand actual miles. Never used a pint of oil. It's a clean car too. Well taken care of. It will be a joy to drive. You won't even know you're pulling anything with that new reflex tow bar. It has a patented action. We've just started using those and they *are* dandies."

An old man in khakis and a blue suit coat came up to open Grady's door. He kept one hand in his pocket and his shoulders were hunched up against the drizzle. He had an orange folder of RJR cigarette papers up in his hatband to keep them dry. They were getting wet.

"This is my brother Tilmon," said Grady. Then he raised his voice and said, "Tilmon, this is Norwood. He's our new driver. He's a good one too. He's a dandy. He's the man who rode the mule around the world."

Tilmon snickered and shook hands with Norwood. There was a frosty glaze on top of his right sleeve where he had been wiping his nose. He took the other hand out of his pocket and gave Norwood a flyer. It said, *Need $$$$$—FAST? Get one of Grady's cost-controlled loans—BY MAIL!* There was a picture of Grady at the bottom holding a fistful of money. *Yes, Grady is ready to lend you up to $950.00—IN THE PRIVACY OF YOUR OWN HOME!*

"How are you?" said Tilmon.

"Just fine," said Norwood.

"Grady is a cutter, ain't he?"

"He sure is."

"How do you like him?"

"I like him all right."

"You do what he says now."

"I will."

"Just to look at Tilmon," said Grady, "you wouldn't

think he was a very astute businessman, would you?"

Norwood looked him over again. "*I* wouldn't have thought it, naw."

"Volume is his middle name. Isn't that right, Tilmon? *I say volume is your middle name.*"

Tilmon said "Tee-hee-hee." His tongue fell out as if to receive a coin.

The second surprise was Miss Phillips. She was sitting in the rain on her suitcase—a handsome blue air travel model—with a newspaper on her head. She was eating peaches from a can with a wooden ice cream spoon. She was a long tall redbone girl. She was wearing a shiny green party dress with shoulder straps, and some open-toed shoes that were just on the point of exploding with toes. She glowered. She looked formidable.

"You run off with the gotdamn car keys and left the doors locked, Fring," she said. Her voice was a piercing whine.

"So I did. I'm sorry about that, Yvonne."

"I'm not *about* to pay for cleaning this dress. Look at it."

"We'll take care of it. Everything will be wonderful. Just keep your shirt on a minute."

"Don't tell me what to do."

"Norwood," said Grady, "this is the extra added attraction. I want you to meet Miss Yvonne Phillips.

53

She hails from Belzoni, Mississippi, by way of New Orleans, the Crescent City. She *is* a dandy. Our talent agency down there is sending her to New York. Since it was convenient I arranged for her to ride up with you. I thought you would welcome the company."

"Yeah. Okay. It's fine with me." He tipped his hat and greeted her.

Miss Phillips glared at Grady. "I hope you don't think I'm gonna ride to New York with this country son of a bitch."

Grady laughed. "She'll cool off, Norwood. It's really me she's mad at, not you. She thought she was going up on a Delta jet. Perhaps you can understand her disappointment. I didn't think you would mind her coming along."

"Naw, it's fine with me. If she wants to. I don't think she wants to."

"She'll get over that."

"I wish Sammy Ortega was here," said Miss Phillips. "He'd break your arm."

"I'd like to see him try it," said Norwood.

"I was talking to Fring, I wasn't talking to you," she said. "But he'd get you too if he felt like it, you bigmouth country son of a bitch. He'd kick your ass into the middle of next week."

"I'd like to see him try it."

54

"You just got through saying that. Don't keep saying the same thing over and over again. Don't you have good sense?"

"You said you was talking to *him* the first time."

"You *peckerwood*."

"That'll be enough," said Grady. "I don't want to hear any more out of you, little lady. Pick up your grip and go over there by the car and wait. I need to have a word with my driver."

"Somebody will get you one of these days, Fring."

"I said hush. Now get your things and move."

She flounced off and yelled at Tilmon and got him to carry her bag.

Grady hitched at his trousers with his wrists and popped his hands together. "Okay, buddy boy, you're gassed up and ready to go. Remember now, the George Washington Bridge, the West Side Drive, the Brooklyn-Battery Tunnel, the Belt Parkway, Exit Twelve, Parsons Street, Arnold's Garage. Follow instructions and watch the signs and you can't miss it. Now listen to this too. You are not authorized to deal with anyone except Arnold. If he's not there then wait on him. The garage is open twenty-four hours and he'll be expecting you late Monday night or early Tuesday morning. He'll take care of everything—up to and including Miss Phillips. She has expense money so she will pay for her own meals. Don't let her pull anything. Of course you may want to work out some personal understanding with her, I don't know. I leave that to your own discretion. In any case remember that we are counting on you to arrive by Tuesday morning at the latest. Got it?"

"I think so."

"Okay. Drive with care now. Watch the other fellow. Stay within the speed limits. Don't get picked up in some little town. Those laws are for our own protection. A car is just like a gun. In the wrong hands it is nothing less than an instrument of death."

The tandem cars splashed down the alley and wheeled around the corner of the ice plant and were gone. A peach can clattered on the street. Grady and Tilmon listened to it until it stopped rolling.

Grady said, "How much did they stick you for those peaches?"

"Thirty-nine cents," said Tilmon.

"They saw you coming, didn't they? That wasn't even a number two can."

"Thirty-nine cents is what they cost."

"I know what they do, they charge you more on Sunday. They jump those prices up on you. They'll all do it. I don't expect we'll run into many grocers in the Kingdom of Heaven, Tilmon."

NORWOOD and Miss Phillips
sped north on U.S. 67. He told her fifteen or twenty
jokes and pointed out amusing signs and discussed
the various construction projects along the way but
she wasn't having any. Except to tell him to slow
down, she absolutely refused to talk. She sat rigid
and sullen far over against her door. Off and on she
pretended to be sleeping. She tried not to move at all
but every few minutes she would scratch, or shift
about on the seat, her shiny dress squeaking, and
each time Norwood would turn to her with a smile.

"You don't have to look over here every time I
move," she said. "Keep your eyes on the road." When
she opened the vent glass she did it very abruptly,
and dropped her hands away like a calf roper in a
rodeo, so as to prevent Norwood from seeing and not-
ing and enjoying the act. As it was, he caught only
the last part of it.

In Little Rock he asked if she would like to stop for a Coke or go to the ladies' room. "I'll let you know when I want to stop, Mr. Big Red." She was in her dozing position again.

"I don't know what you're so mad about," he said, "but we got a long ways to go yet. We could make a right nice trip out of it if you wouldn't act that way. I would like to be your good friend, Laverne."

She didn't even open her eyes. "Yeah, I bet you would. My name is not Laverne, it's *Yuh-von*. I don't want *you* calling me anything."

On they rode in hostile silence through the rice fields and the one-stoplight towns of eastern Arkansas. The rain let up some but the trucks were still throwing up muddy slop on the windshield. Grady was right about the reflex tow bar. It was a little wonder. There was no bucking and yawing on the curves, even at high speed. He was right about the Olds too. It was clean and fast and powerful. The tinted glass made it snug inside. Everything worked, the radio, the clock, even the windshield squirters. Norwood could have driven that 98 Oldsmobile through all eternity and never stopped.

They stopped in De Valls Bluff to get some peaches. Miss Phillips paid for them but she wouldn't get out of the car. Norwood had a barbecue sandwich and a Nugrape. They ate in the car and pressed on.

Just before they got to Brinkley Norwood broke the silence with a shout and hit the brakes. "Hey look at that!" Miss Phillips bolted and her red knees bumped against the dashboard. Some of the peach juice splashed from the can and ran down her legs. "What is it!" she said. "Where!"

"You missed him," said Norwood. "There was a possum back there crawling through that fence. He looked like a big old slow rat."

Miss Phillips was frantically daubing at her legs with wads of Kleenex. "You son of a bitch!"

Norwood hit the brakes again. "You want to go back and see him?"

More juice erupted from the can, and this time two or three golden Del Monte slivers with it. They stuck on her dress and made dark growing splotches. "What the hell is wrong with you, fellow!" she shrieked. "Look at what you've done! You think I want to see a possum crawling through a fence!"

"He's already through the fence," said Norwood. "He's back there in that field now looking for something. He's probably looking for some chow."

"You're the biggest peckerwood son of a bitch in the world!"

"I don't like that kind of talk out of a girl, Laverne. How would you like your mama to hear you talking like that?"

Miss Phillips had no answer. She quite unexpectedly broke into tears. She did not cry loud but she cried dramatically and long. It went on for miles, the snuffling and the little chirping noises. Norwood considered and dismissed seven or eight things to say. They were on the approaches to the Memphis Bridge when he went back to the first one.

"I didn't aim to make you cry. I'm sorry I brought that up about your mama."

"That's not what I'm crying about, stud."

"I'll just keep my mouth shut from now on. No matter what I see."

Miss Phillips wiped her eyes. Some of her fire was gone. "I wish I was in Calumet City, Illinois. I don't want to go to New York. Sammy Ortega is a bartender in Calumet City and he could get me a job there easy."

"Is he the one that's gonna whup everybody?"

"Sammy may not look very big in his street clothes," she said, "but he can press two hundred pounds over his head. He can speak four languages too."

"What are they?"

"What?"

"What are the languages?"

"English and Spanish and I don't know what all. Italian."

"What is he, a Mexican?"

"He's Spanish."

"A lot of Mexicans are named Jesus."

"What's wrong with that?"

"Nothing. I thought maybe it was something you didn't know."

The traffic was heavy on the bridge. Norwood was on the inside, fast lane and he was twisting his neck trying to get a look at the three big oil barges that were chugging along downstream in the muddy Mississippi far below. A small wooden sign in the center of the bridge said SHELBY CO., TENN.

"You just crossed the state line," said Miss Phillips. "Now they can send you to the Federal pen." Norwood brought the cars to a skidding stop. Miss Phillips was thrown forward and her head slammed against the windshield. "You can't stop here, you fool!" A white station wagon smashed into the back of the Pontiac. Miss Phillips was thrown backward this time, from the neck up, and her head slammed against the center post. The driver of the station wagon had jumped out and he was running for Norwood and shouting. He had a bloody head. Norwood put the accelerator on the floor and the Oldsmobile sat down hard and shot off again with rubber squealing. Norwood yelled back at the man with the bloody head. "I'll see you in town!" Miss Phillips was crying again. There was a big swelling knot on her forehead. She was holding her head and rocking back and forth on the seat. Norwood said, "I got to get out of here." They were forty miles from Memphis and passing through Covington, Tennessee, before he said another word.

"Grady told me a lie."

"What did you think he would do?" said the red-eyed Miss Phillips. She was holding a wet Kleenex on her forehead. "I feel sorry for anybody like you. You are the peckerwood of all peckerwoods."

"I'm getting tired of that peckerwood business."

"Well, stop calling me Laverne then."

"I don't see how anybody from Belzoni, Mississippi, can call anybody else a peckerwood. How big is Belzoni? . . . It couldn't be too big. You'd hear more about it if it was."

"For your information, I spent a lot of time in New Orleans, *Mr. Red on the Head.* I count that as my home."

"It's *not* your home though."

"If you live someplace a long time you can count it as your home."

"Naw you can't. . . . You could live in Hong Kong for seventy-five years and Belzoni would still be your home."

"Don't sit there and tell *me* what *my* home is."

"I *am* telling you. Somebody needs to tell you."

"I hope a cop stops you. I really do. They'll have you locked up down there in that Atlanta pen so fast it'll make your head swim. You're sitting over there right now just scared to death."

There was some truth in this. It was a tough problem. Norwood would think about it for a while and rest for a while. It was like looking at the sun. He waited on something to come to him, some plan. What road was he on? Where was the gas gauge on this oversize jet plane dashboard? Half a tank? Where had he stopped? Somewhere. The man had checked him out on the revoked credit card list. Like he was somebody who shouldn't have a credit card. Anyway, nothing much could happen as long as they were moving along like this. Darkness fell and the problem lost much of its urgency. Norwood's mind was soon on other things.

They made only one stop in Kentucky, a peach stop in some little place just across the Ohio River, and, lost in their own thoughts, said nothing to each other until they were approaching Evansville, Indiana. The radio had been droning on for hours untended and a gospel hour was in progress when Miss Phillips reached over and turned the dial.

Norwood said, "What are you doing?"

"I'm trying to get WWL in New Orleans," she said.

"You can pick it up a long ways late at night. I want to hear *Moonglow with Martin.*"

Norwood pushed her hand away and regained the gospel program. "I was listening to that."

"We been hearing preachers all night." She changed stations again.

Norwood turned it back. "This one is explaining why they don't have any pianos in the Church of Christ. I want to hear him. Don't put your hand on the radio again."

"Well, I *don't* want to hear him."

"I do though."

"You're not the boss."

"I'm the boss of this car."

Miss Phillips fumed. The preacher went on uninterrupted. In closing he said he was prepared to pay ten thousand dollars cash to anyone who could show him scriptural authority for having a musical instrument in a church.

"I wisht I knew more about the Bible," said Norwood.

He considered and mused on the offer for some little time. "I wonder if he would really pay you? . . . It looks like he'd have to if he said it over the air. . . . Well . . . I'd whup his ass if he didn't."

"I'm tired of this preaching," said Miss Phillips.

"Hank Snow's son is a preacher," said Norwood.

"The Reverend Jimmie Rodgers Snow. He's got him a church off over there in Tennessee somewhere."

"I want to hear some music."

"What church do you belong to, Laverne?"

"None of your business."

"The Church of God?"

"I belong to just as good a church as you do. Probably a lot better one."

"Well, maybe you do and maybe you don't. I belong to the Third Baptist Church in Ralph, Texas, and I'm proud of it."

"I figured you would belong to the Fourth Baptist Church."

"They don't have one in Ralph."

"That's why you don't belong to it."

"The Missionary Baptists, they all go over to Hooks. I think the Free Will Baptists just get together at somebody's house. We're gonna have air conditioning in the new annex if they ever get it finished. Do they have air conditioning in the Pentecost Church in Belzoni?"

"My church comes under the head of my business."

"If I was a Holy Roller I wouldn't be ashamed of it. I would be proud of it."

"I would too, if I was a Holy Roller."

"Only half the people that *are* in the church are saved."

"Has that car back there got a radio in it?"

Norwood checked it out in the mirror. "It's got a aerial, yeah."

"Well, stop and let me go get in it. I want to hear *Moonglow with Martin.*"

"You can't ride back there. It'll look funny. Some cop is liable to stop us."

"I don't care. If you don't stop I'll holler out at the next cop I see. At the next anybody."

"All right, change the station. Get whatever you want on this radio."

"I want to get back in that other car. I want to hear it on *that* radio now."

Norwood pulled over and stopped. He got the fiber envelope out of the glove compartment and gave her the keys to the Pontiac. "Here. All you're gonna do is run that battery down and probably get us arrested." They rode into Evansville like that, Norwood in his car, Miss Phillips in hers. There was nothing doing in downtown Evansville. Night lights were burning in the stores but the streets were still and deserted. Miss Phillips began blatting her horn. It boomed and rang and echoed, and Norwood's first impulse was to step on it, but he stopped. Miss Phillips got back in the Olds.

"What's wrong with you now?"

"I want some coffee," said Miss Phillips. "I don't

like it back there in that car with nobody driving it."

At an all-night diner on the edge of town they sat on stools and had coffee and cold sugary fried pies. Miss Phillips was morose. She had knots on her head fore and aft, and her legs were sticky with dried peach juice. The green party dress looked awful. Norwood snapped at the counter girl for putting cream in his coffee. She said she didn't know where he was from but if you wanted it black you had to say so. He told her he was from a place where they let you put your own cream in your coffee. From little syrup pitchers with spring lids.

Miss Phillips, wistfully eating her fried pie, was not listening to this byplay. "Sammy would get me a job right off," she said. "But I wouldn't want Grady to know where I was. I guess you would tell him."

"I wouldn't tell him what time it was," said Norwood. "After the way he done me."

"He's a disbarred lawyer and he knows a thousand ways to get you in trouble. I'd be afraid you would tell him where I went."

"Naw, I said I wouldn't. I wisht you *would* go on. It would be a load off my mind."

"I'm sorry I talked so ugly to you, Red. Why don't you let me have one of those cars?"

Norwood put the keys on the counter. "I don't want anything more to do with *you* or them cars.

Take both of 'em, Laverne, and go on. You can give one to Sammy. Tell him hello for me."

"I can't drive but one. You'll have to unhook 'em."

It was a job getting the reflex tow bar off. All he had was a pair of pliers. Somebody with big shoulders and a four-way lug wrench had jammed those nuts down to stay. It was no use, not with pliers. He kicked it and beat it with a rock. Finally he attacked it with a jack handle and chanted *"This time . . . this time . . . this time . . ."* until it broke loose. Miss Phillips had no goodbye for Norwood. She took the Oldsmobile without a word or a wave and roared off into the Midwestern night flinging driveway gravel. The tow bar, its ingenious patented action now so much junk, was dragging along behind, bouncing on the highway and kicking up sparks.

Norwood drove the Pontiac out past the last lights of town and turned off on a dirt road. He turned off that road onto a two-rut road and then into what looked like a blackberry patch. He gunned it through the thicket and over arm-size saplings, giving the Indiana forest folk a scare, until it hit some bigger trees and stopped. He forced his door open against the bushes and got out and looked around. This was not such a smart idea. What would a car be doing here? Somebody would report it first thing tomorrow. He tried to back it out but the rear wheels were sunk hub deep in sand and wouldn't rock free. Well, he was tired of fooling with it. He took a towel from his bag and gave the door handles and the interior a good wiping down. It had been a proud day when he had given the Marine Corps his fingerprints and now they were up there in some drawer in Washington waiting to do him in. He ran his hand under the seat to see if he had left any clues. Any peanuts or guitar picks or things they could look at through a microscope. It smelled a little of Miss Phillips down there. He burned the fiber envelope and its contents and then he zipped up his bag and slung the guitar across his back and walked a good three miles back toward town to the nearest filling station. He stood on the highway under the station's harsh blue mercury lights and swatted bugs out of his face.

THE SUN WAS COMING UP before he got a ride. It was a bread truck. The driver was a round sloping man who was wearing an official bread hat with a sunburst medallion and a T-shirt that was so thin hairs were breaking through it. A bulldozer watch fob lay on his lap. Norwood thought at first he had rubber bands around his wrists. They were fat and dimpled like baby wrists.

"This is against the rules," said the bread man, "but I just can't pass a man up. My wife says I'm too kind for my own good."

"Well, I sure appreciate it," said Norwood. "I was getting pretty tired."

The truck was a delivery model with no passenger seat and Norwood had to sit on a wooden bread box. He laid the guitar across his knees. There was a bad shimmy in the front wheels and this made the guitar bounce and hum.

"I'll have to make a few stops, but a man begging a ride ought to be glad to get whatever he can."

"This is fine. I appreciate it too."

"Have you got a dollar to help on the gas?"

Norwood gave him a dollar. "Do you have to pay for your own gas?"

The man looked straight ahead. "Sometimes I do."

"How much does a job like this pay?" said Norwood. "A bread job?"

"Well, it don't pay as much as heavy construction work but you don't have to work as hard neither. I used to drive a D-8 cat till I hurt my back. Didn't do anything while I was on workmen's compensation. Just went to the show all the time. I like *The Road Runner*."

"Yeah, I do too."

"I could watch that scutter for an hour."

"I believe I could too."

The bread man began to rumble with quiet laughter. "That coyote or whatever he is, a wolf or something, every time he gets up on a clift or somewhere with a new plan, why the Road Runner comes along on some skates or has him some new invention like a rocket or a big wrecker's ball and just busts that coyote a good one." He laughed some more, then fell into repose. In a minute or two his face clouded with a darker memory. "Noveltoons are not any good at all," he said. "It's usually a shoemaker and a bunch of damn mice singing. When one of them comes on I get up and go get me a sack of corn or something."

They shimmied on down the road. At the first stop, a roadside grocery store, Norwood got a quart of milk and had the grocer make him a couple of baloney and cheese sandwiches with mayonnaise. He leaned on the meat box and ate and watched the bread man do his stuff. The bread man carried old bread out and brought new bread in. He squatted down and arranged it on the rack. Norwood noticed that he was poking finger holes in the competitors' loaves. Their eyes met, just for a second, and the bread man looked away. He tried to recover by doing peculiar things with his hands, as though he had a funny way of arranging bread. Norwood was not deceived. The bread man had no gift for pantomime and he did not seem to consider that from a range of eight or nine feet it is easy enough to tell whether someone is or is not punching holes in bread.

He said nothing about it and neither did Norwood. But back on the road the guilty knowledge hung heavy over the conversation. The bread man tried to get something going again. He asked Norwood if that was a Gibson guitar, but before Norwood could answer the man said, "My whole family is musical. Some families are like that. My sister used to play trombone solos in church. Daddy played the accordion and we would all sing. He could really play that thing. And didn't know note one."

"They're hard to beat," said Norwood, agreeably. "I like to hear a good accordion."

"Daddy passed on two days after Labor Day of 1951," said the bread man, forestalling any suggestion that they go hear the old gentleman play.

They picked up another hitchhiker. This one was carrying a sack of garden tomatoes. Norwood made room for him on the box. The man was grateful and deeply apologetic and he insisted on shaking their hands. Norwood had never seen a man so happy to get a ride. "This sure is nice of you," he kept saying.

"I'm not supposed to do it," said the bread man. "I just don't like to pass anybody up. Might need a ride myself sometime. How far are you going?"

"I'm going on in to Indianapolis. My wife is in the hospital there. She doesn't have any sweat glands."

"I never had a cold in my life," said the bread man.

"It was sure nice of you to stop like that. A lot of people are scared of hitchhikers. I guess you can't blame 'em."

"Have you got a dollar to help on the gas?"

73

The man looked frightened. "No sir, I sure don't. All I got is sixty cents and I was going to get my wife some ice cream with that. That's why I'm thumbing. I'm supposed to get a little check Friday."

The bread man stopped the truck and nodded at Norwood. "Well, it wouldn't be fair to him if I let you ride. He paid his dollar."

"I don't care," said Norwood. "It's all right with me."

But the bread man made no move to get the truck going again. He looked impassively into the distance.

"I tell you what, if you'll let me ride I'll try to do something nice for somebody else on down the road. I'll return the favor that way. I'll do somebody else a good deed and tell them to pass it on. . . . Maybe it'll go all the way around the world. . . ."

It was no use. The man got out with his sack of tomatoes after riding fifty yards. "Well . . . thank you anyway. . . . I'm sorry . . . if it was Friday I would have the money." He was pained at having caused trouble. Everybody was right but him.

The bread man drove away and glanced at Norwood to see how he was taking it. "He wasn't going to do anything for anybody down the road. That was a load of crap."

"I think he would have," said Norwood. "You ought to let him ride."

"You think so, huh? Why didn't you pay his dollar?"

"I didn't think about that. I guess I could have. . . . Let's go back and get him."

"I'm not running a bus service. Anyway, I didn't like his personality."

"You should of let him ride."

"Maybe *you* don't like *my* personality."

"I don't know you very well."

"Maybe you think I have personality trouble."

"I just don't know you."

"That's not any kind of answer. Why don't you say what you think? You think I don't know that some people don't like me because of my personality? I know that. My wife wants me to take a course. They're giving one at the hotel next week that's supposed to help you in sales work. It makes people like you."

"Why don't you take it?"

"What do you know about it? You're just a hitch-hiker begging rides."

"Well . . ."

"You saw me back there roughing up that bread, didn't you?"

"Yeah, I did."

"I got nothing to hide. *They* started it. What do you want me to do?"

"It's none of my business."

"You mighty right it's not. The Vita-White guys *step* on my bread. Mash it all in with their feet. No telling what kind of germs is on their shoes. They don't care. A little child's death don't mean anything to them."

"I believe I'll get out along here, just anywhere."

"I'm going on in to town."

"I believe I'll get out anyway."

"That's fine with me. I'll be glad to get rid of you. You're not friendly."

He pulled over on the shoulder and stopped short. Norwood said, "much oblige," and got out.

"You need to do something about your personality, hitchhiker. That's what you need."

"What *you* need is about forty dollars worth of front end work on this truck," said Norwood. "Some new kingpins."

"I hope don't nobody pick you up."

"No use in you hoping that. Somebody will."

At a pool hall in Indianapolis a rack boy with a Junior Tracy haircut and a good opinion of himself told Norwood that if he was going to New York he wouldn't bother with hitchhiking, he would go out to the Pennsylvania yards and catch him a freight train. Norwood shot snooker with him most of the afternoon and lost $2.75, then downed two chili dogs and went out to the rail yards and wandered around in the dark.

He had never done this before. There were tracks and more tracks and empty flatcars and switch engines banging around and trains coming in and trains going out. The thing was to ask somebody. He walked over to the station and talked to a Negro man in coveralls who was pushing a mail buggy. The man pointed out a freight train that was being made up for Philadelphia and said be careful. Norwood circled all the way around to the end of the train—instead of just crawling over a coupling—and came back up the other side where it was darker. He walked along like an inspector giving all the boxcar hatches a shake, and finally found one he liked. It was a faded blue L & N car with a banged-up door that wouldn't close all the way. No one could lock that door on him. He slid it back and struck a match and looked in. Big sacks of flour, hundred-pounders, were stacked high at each end of the car, almost to the roof. There was an open space in the middle of the car. He pushed his bag and guitar in and climbed in after them.

It was pitch-dark inside and hot, close, airless. Well, he would be riding at night. It would be cooler when they started moving. The floor was nothing but splinters. He wished he had a flashlight. It was probably dangerous striking matches with all that flour. He pulled some of the sacks down and fashioned himself a place to sleep. It looked like a nest for some bird that never lived on this earth. He slipped his boots off and settled back into it and tipped his hat over his eyes range style. No. Better be ready for a fast move. Better put the boots back on. Like getting caught by the gooks in one of those sleeping bags that zipped only halfway down. A suicide bag. He ate a dime Payday and then peeled an orange and ate it and lay there quiet and watchful in that ghostly Pillsbury darkness until the train moved.

It started with a clanging jerk. Norwood was half asleep. He turned on his side and adjusted his hat. Drops of sweat ran across his back and tickled. He was sweating like a hog. Did hogs sweat? No. That's why they like mudholes. Mules did, and horses. Out in the sun they had shiny wet skins. He tried to remember what a hog's skin looked like out in the sun. He couldn't remember seeing a hog in the sun. For any length of time. Hogs didn't have to work. Had anybody ever tried to *make* one work? Maybe they tried it a long time ago in history, and just gave up. And told their sons not to bother with it any more. Better not leave the guitar out loose like that. All kinds of folks riding trains. He looped the shoulder cord around his wrist a couple of times. The bag was under his head, safe. Everything was secured. The head is secured. Some boot standing there at the door with a swab at port arms trying to keep you out. Even when it was secured for regimental inspection they had to keep one bowl and one urinal open. Everybody knew that. Why did they keep on trying to pull that swab on you? Norwood dozed and woke and blew flour out of his nose and slept and groaned and dreamed crazy dreams about Miss Phillips. The train stopped and started all night long. It seemed to last about three days.

The train was slowing for the block in Philadelphia when Norwood suddenly awoke. He was asleep one second and wide awake the next. A thin wall of sunlight was coming through the doorway crack, with a lot of stuff dancing around in it. Something was wrong. It was his feet. He felt air on his feet. He sat up and there wasn't anything on them except a pair of J. C. Penney Argyles. Somebody had taken his thirty-eight-dollar stovepipe boots right off his feet. *"Son of a bitch!"* He got up and climbed over the floor and pulled sacks this way and that way but there was no one to be found, and no boots.

Soon it was so thick with flour dust in the car that he had to slam one of the doors back and stick his head out for air. The trouble was, two of the sacks had broken. After he caught his breath he dragged them over and pushed them out. The second one snagged on the bad door and hung there for a moment blowing flour up in his face. Then he began *flinging* sacks out, good ones, till he got a cramp in his neck.

The train entered the yard with long blats from the diesel horn and as it lurched in for a stop Norwood grabbed up his gear and bailed out in his sock feet. It stung. He squatted there and looked long and hard up and down the train, through the wheels, to see if anybody else was jumping off. Nobody. He dusted himself off, whacking his trousers with his hat, and decided to do some backtracking along the roadbed.

He couldn't walk far. The rocks and clinkers hurt his feet and he sat down on a stack of crossties to put on another layer of socks. While he was sitting there smoking a cigarette he saw two men in the distance coming up the tracks. One of them was wearing a luminous orange jacket. It was blinding. He might have had some job that required him to be easily spotted by aircraft. Norwood waited.

The one with the jacket was a tall whiskery man. He was also wearing a St. Louis Cardinal's baseball cap. By his side, stepping smartly along with a knotty walking stick, was a short angry little man with a knapsack on his back. He was covered from head to toe with flour, except right around his eyes and mouth.

"What happened to you, neighbor?" said Norwood.

"You should of seen it," said the man with the Cardinal cap. "Some thug was throwing flour out of a boxcar and Eugene here was walking along not thinking about anything when one of 'em hit him. One of them sacks."

"Was he hurt?"

"Well, it didn't hurt him, but it didn't help him none either."

He wanted to stop and talk about it some more, the sexagenarian Cardinal, but his short chum kept moving. He didn't even glance at Norwood. He looked like a man who was going somewhere to report something. Norwood had to run around in front of him to stop him. "Hey wait a minute. I better have a look in that pack. Somebody got my boots last night." The flour man looked up and fixed Norwood with two evil red eyes, but said nothing. The Cardinal did not like the turn things had taken. Maybe he could explain it again.

"We don't know anything about any boots. Eugene got hit with some flour, that's all. Some thug was throwing it off the train. I got hit with a mail pouch myself once but it wasn't anything like this. This was like a flour bomb went off."

Norwood moved around behind the flour man and reached up to undo the straps on the knapsack. With that, the flour man went into action. He was like lightning. He was a tiger. He spun around and hit Norwood on the arms three or four times with his stick and when it broke he popped Norwood in the mouth with a straight left and then he jumped up on his back and stuck there like a small white bear. The knapsack on *his* back was like a yet smaller bear.

"Look out! Look out!" the Cardinal was saying. He had jumped back well clear of the action. "Turn him loose, Eugene! He's another Hitler!"

Norwood was dancing around jabbing at the man with his elbows trying to shake him off. He backed him up and bumped him against the crossties. The man's ankles were locked together in front and Norwood broke them loose but the man had a hold on his neck that wouldn't quit. "You better get him off before I bust his head open," said Norwood, stopping to rest a minute. He was breathing hard. His upper lip was bloody.

The Cardinal moved in a little closer. Maybe something could be worked out now. "Eugene don't weigh very much, does he?" he said.

"I still don't want him on my back."

"He's light enough to be a jockey. Of course he's way too old."

"How long does he generally hang on?"

"I don't know. I never seen him do that before. . . . They say a snapping turtle won't let go till it thunders. That's what I've heard. I never was bit by a turtle. My oldest sister was bit by a mad fox. They didn't have any screens on their house and it come in a window one night and nipped her on the leg like a little dog will do. They carried that fox's head on in to Birmingham in some ice and said it was mad and she had to take all them shots. She said she hoped she never did get bit by nair another one."

Norwood kicked his feet forward and fell backward on the flour man and they hit the deck in a puff of white. The flour man was squeezed between Norwood and the pack and it knocked the wind out of him. He made a lung noise like *gunh!* He turned loose and sat up and brushed himself off a little, still defiant but not fighting any more. Norwood opened the knapsack and poked around in it. There were rolled-up clothes and a cast-iron skillet and pie pans and a can of Granger and cotton blankets and copies of *True Police Cases* and a mashed store cake and crackers and cans of chili and lima beans and an insulated plastic cup and a bottle of 666 Tonic and a clock and an old five-shot top-breaking .32 revolver with a heavy fluted barrel and taped-on grips. No boots. But in one of the side pouches he did find some shoes.

They were old-timers' high tops with elastic strips on the sides. Norwood tried them on and walked around flexing them and looking at them in profile. They were plenty loose. Eugene didn't have feet, he had flippers. Norwood said, "I'll give you two dollars for these dudes."

"Those are my house shoes," said Eugene, speaking for the first time and the last.

"A man comes along and needs some shoes, you ought to want to help him. You already got some good shoes on."

"Eugene doesn't want to sell his house shoes," said the Cardinal.

"*You* stay out of this," said Norwood.

"You international thug. You're just like Hitler and Tojo wrapped up into one."

Norwood tried Eugene once more. "Look, you can get another pair of these dudes easy for six bits at the Goodwill Store. I'm offering you two dollars. What about me? I don't have any shoes. I lost some thirty-eight-dollar boots last night. They took 'em right off my feet. They didn't give *me* anything."

"You better give Tojo what he wants, Eugene. He'll

terrorize you if you don't. That's the way he does business."

"Don't call me Tojo any more."

"This is a free country, *thug*. You can call people anything you want to. Can't you, Eugene?"

Norwood rolled the two dollar bills into a cylinder and pushed it into Eugene's shirt pocket. "I ought not to give you anything. Jumping up on people's backs. They'll put you in a home somewhere if you don't watch out."

NORWOOD paid his fare and rode a commuter special in to New York. He sat in the smoking section in a green padded seat that faced crossways and took up both armrests with his elbows. He bought some coffee in a paper cup with handles, and a heavy cakelike doughnut that stuck in the throat. It had an unpleasant spicy taste. "You want the rest of this?" he said to the man sitting by him.

"No, thanks."

"I didn't put my hands on it."

"Thanks but no."

Norwood placed it in the chrome ashtray between them. The man glanced down at it. In a minute or two he did it again. "I didn't see any other place to put it," said Norwood. He picked it up and put in his empty cup and held it. His hands were cold. Too much smoking? He flexed his fingers and made the joints pop. A bow-tied man across the aisle, not much himself but maybe some pretty girl's father, was watching him. Norwood stared back. The man looked up at the light fixture on the ceiling to calculate its dimensions and efficiency. There were no girls on the train, no women at all, only these clean men. They bathed every day, every morning. He caught another one looking at him down the way. He *was* a mess, no doubt about it. The sole of one shoe was flopping and he had B.O. pretty bad. His red beard was beginning to bristle and there were patches of flour like dirty snow on his back where Eugene had been. One day Eugene would let somebody have it with that .32. Get a face full of hot powder himself, with that loose cylinder.

He had some more coffee at a stand-up counter in Penn Station and the people there looked at him too, but not for long because they had to get back to their newspapers. He picked up his change and looked at it. "Hey wait a minute," he called to the girl. She had black hair piled up high and dark tiger eyes. She came back and gave the counter a quick wipe with a blue sponge that had one cornflake riding on the stern. She looked at the dime and nickel in his hand. That was right. People watched furtively over their papers. This guy with the hat was going to start something.

"What is it?" said the girl.

"I guess you didn't hear the radio this morning," he said.

"I don't gitcha."

He pointed at the fifteen cents. "The weatherman said no change today."

"Oh fer Chrissakes."

Somebody on the other side of the plastic orange juice vat said, "What did he say?" and somebody else said, "I couldn't hear it." They all went back to their papers. Whatever it was, it was over.

A friendly airman third class found Joe William's number in the Manhattan directory and Norwood tried to give him a quarter but he wouldn't take it. He brought his bag and guitar into the booth with him and dialed. The phone started to ring, then made an unsatisfactory noise and a recorded voice came through to say the number had been disconnected. He got his dime back and dialed the operator. After a short discussion she passed him on to a supervisor.

"That number has been disconnected, sir," said the supervisor.

"Yeah, that othern told me that. Do you know if he's gone home or what?"

"We don't have that information."

"I thought he might of left word with somebody in case somebody needed to get aholt of him."

"No sir, we don't have that kind of information."

"I guess you can't keep up with everybody, can you?"

"No sir, we can't."

"Uh-huh. Well. Goodbye."

"Goodbye."

He washed up in the men's room but it didn't help much. What he needed was a bath and a shave. His hair was stiff and in places it hurt when he mashed down on it in a certain way. This was no place to shave, worse than a barracks head. Traffic and flushing and people combing their hair behind you and not enough flat surfaces around the bowl to put your stuff on. The faucets had strong springs in them so you couldn't let the water run. A man bumped him and said "Sorry" and Norwoood quickly checked his billfold and made sure the hip pocket was buttoned. This was the kind of place pickpockets liked. Those boogers had quick hands. Be all in your clothes and you wouldn't know it. He dried off under a hot air blower.

Outside, a porter pointed him toward Times Square. As he made his way up Seventh Avenue a man with puffy eyes (dope fiend?) stopped him and tried to sell him a four-color ball-point pen for a dollar. Norwood brushed him off. What did they think, that he was somebody who would buy something like that on the street? No telling what they were thinking, the way he looked. That he would be amazed at a lot of things. Like *Tarzan's New York Adventure.*

He looked at the movie posters on both sides of Forty-second Street and had a glass of beer and some giant corrugated French fries. The windows were full of many good buys in transistor radios and field glasses. Did any one live upstairs over the movie theaters? He saw himself on television at Robert Ripley's Believe It or Not Odditorium, and looked at all the curios downstairs, believing most of them but not believing the one about Marshal W. M. Pitman of Wharton, Texas, shooting a bullet right into a crook's gun in 1932. Still, there was the gun, and why would they make it up? Across the street he watched a man with a beanie at a sewing machine. The man was talking like Donald Duck and sewing names on other beanies. *Stella* and *Fred* and *Ernie.* His workmanship was good. How did he get that job? What did it pay? Being able to sew names and talk like Donald Duck. He walked up as far as Fifty-ninth Street, where things began to peter out, then came back. There was a man in a Mr. Peanut outfit in front of the Planters place but he was not giving out sample nuts, he was just walking back and forth. The Mr. Peanut casing looked hot. It looked thick enough to give protection against small arms fire.

"Do they pay you by the hour or what?" Norwood said to the monocled peanut face.

"Yeah, by the hour," said a wary, muffled voice inside.

"I bet that suit is heavy."

"It's not all that heavy. I just started this morning."

"How much do you get a hour?"

"You ast a lot of questions, don't you?"

"Do you take the suit home with you?"

"No, I put it on down here. At the shop."

"The one in Dallas gives out free nuts."

"I don't know anything about that. They didn't say anything to me about it."

"He don't give you many, just two or three cashews."

"I don't know anything about that. I work at the post office at night."

"Well, I'll see you sometime, Mr. Peanut. You take it easy."

"Okay. You too."

A woman in the Times Square Information Center, about forty but with a smooth powdered neck he wouldn't have minded biting, gave him a subway map and told him that the best way to get to the East Eleventh Street address was to take the BMT to Union Square, then change to the Fourteenth Street-

Canarsie line going east and get off at First Avenue.
It was impossible to remember. On his way to the
subway entrance he stopped at a shoeshine parlor to
ask again. Or it was not so much a parlor as a notch
in the wall with room for only one chair and the shine
man himself, who was small and dark and aproned.

"Say—"

"Beat it, fellow," said the shine man, not looking up
from his work. "I don't have time to answer questions."

"I just wanted to know—"

"You wanna know something, ask a cop. They get
paid for it. I pay two hundred dollars a month for this
rathole and at twenty cents a shine that means I got
to shine two thousand individual shoes just to pay the
rent."

Norwood forgot his own problem at once. "You're
not figuring your tips in on that?"

"I don't have time to talk, fellow. Beat it, okay?
If I was on the city payroll it would be different.
Everybody thinks I'm on the city payroll."

"You're trying to make it sound like you have to
shine more shoes than you really do. Why don't you
figure your tips in on it?"

The shine man stood up and put one fist on his hip
and did a Mediterranean fast burn. "You can't figure
it that way, Mr. Smart Guy. You gotta figure it on

your base rate, which is twenty cents. A lotta smart guys think they know more about my business than I do."

The man in the chair put down his magazine. "Look, I'm in kind of a hurry," he said.

"Sure, you're in a hurry," said the shine man. "*I'm* in a hurry, everybody in the *world* is in a hurry except this smart guy that has time to go down the street telling everybody how to run their business. How can I work with a smart guy standing over my shoulder telling me how to run my business? The answer is—*I can't.*"

"Leave him alone, buddy," said the man in the chair.

"Go bother Mayor Wagner," said the shine man. "He needs advice. Tell him how to run the city. He's on the city payroll. Don't bother me, bother somebody on the city payroll."

The subway was cleaner and more brightly lighted than Norwood had expected, and it moved faster. He jostled his way forward to the front car and looked through the glass with his hands cupped around his face. He was disappointed to find the tunnel so roomy. Only a very fat man could be trapped in it with a train coming. The air smelled of electricity and dirt.

In one of the pedestrian tunnels at the Union Square stop a man was stretched out on the concrete having a fit and forcing people to step around him in the narrow passageway. Norwood watched him as he gave a few terminal jerks and a long sigh. He knew he should look to see if the man had swallowed his tongue, the way they used to have to do with that Eubanks boy in the fifth grade, but he didn't want to put his finger in the man's mouth unless he had to. It was all right for doctors. They didn't care where they put their hands. He lifted the man by the armpits and propped him against the wall. The man rolled his eyes. His legs were rubbery and he couldn't stand alone.

"You want some water?" said Norwood.

"Water? Yeah."

"Well . . . I don't have any. How about a cigarette?"

"You can't smoke down here."

"What's wrong with you?"

"I'll be all right in a minute."

A woman with some packages stopped and inquired and Norwood told her to go see if she could find somebody. She said she would tell a transit policeman. Norwood waited. Without the blockage people rushed along now in a steady stream. No policeman came. A foot brushed the guitar and made it ring. The man closed his eyes and took a nap standing there. No policeman. Norwood reached out into the stream and grabbed a man's arm, a dapper man in a neat metallic suit.

"Hold this fellow up a minute."

The man jumped and did as he was told. Then he said, "Hey, what is this, you?"

Norwood was picking up his gear. "Somebody's coming to get him. They're on the way."

"Where are you going? What do you think you're doing? You can't detain me like this. I'm an officer of the court. I've got to get downtown."

"We all got to catch trains. I can't be down here helping folks out all day myself. I don't even live here."

"I won't be put in a false position, you. This is a false position."

"I got to go."

Norwood found the Canarsie line with no trouble but on the train he let his mind wander and the next thing he knew he was under the river, and then in Brooklyn. Arnold. Was he on the phone to Grady? He crossed over the platform and doubled back on another train and this time he stood by the doors all the way. Daylight again. First Avenue and Fourteenth. Tenements and garbage cans. This was where people lived in New York. Leo Gorcey and his pals working up a plan in the candy store. Huntz Hall messing up everything. *Satch.*

It was a short walk to the address on Eleventh Street. On the sidewalk in front of the place some shirtless Puerto Rican boys were roasting marshmallows over a smoldering mattress.

Norwood stopped and looked at the tenement number and rested the guitar on his foot. "You boys having a big time?"

"It's a campfire," said one. He was wearing huge comic sunglasses and had his head tilted back to keep them on. He offered Norwood a blackened marshmallow from the end of a straightened-out coat hanger.

"I believe I'd rather have one right out of the sack. They ain't gonna taste like anything cooked over hair." He reached for the cellophane package but another boy grabbed it off the stoop. Norwood let it pass. "You boys need to get you some wood. You need a wood far for these dudes."

"We don't have any wood."

"Go down at the store and get you a apple box. They'll let you have one. Pine would be better than what you got here."

The boy who grabbed the marshamallows pointed at the guitar. "Can you play that?"

"Yeah and I'm liable to get it out just any minute and sing a song. Do yall know a old boy name Joe William Reese?"

Nobody said anything.

"I know this is where he lives. I got it on a piece of paper."

Nobody said anything.

"When will you play that guitar?" said the grabber.

"It's hard to say. I might not play it all now."

"Marie has a guitar. She knows a hundred songs."

"She don't know that many."

"She does too."

"I don't know but one myself. It's about a squirrel. He lived out in the woods and every time he would get something good his friends would be hungry and they would come around and want some. They'd say, 'Hey, squirrel, let me have a bite of that Clark bar.' And the squirrel, he would say, real mean, 'Naw! I'm on eat it all myself! It's good too!' And pretty soon out there in the woods they were all calling him the stingy squirrel and he didn't have any more friends to play with."

The boys looked at Norwood.

"Well, it's more what you would call a story than a song," he said. "There's a good lesson in it."

He examined a row of mailboxes in the foyer and Joe William's name was there all right, although it had been penciled over # 2. The hall was dark and there were dust balls that the broom had missed. They rolled along like miniature tumbleweeds. Norwood struck a match and found # 2 the first shot. He stood outside the door for a moment. There was movement inside. He unzipped the guitar and without tuning up he hit one loud nylon chord and sang:

> *There'll be smoke on the water*
> *And the land and the sea*
> *When our army and navy*
> *Overtake the enemee . . .*

A dog started barking upstairs, a little scrappy one, and some woman took it up and started yelling down. The stairwell echoed with female Spanish abuse. The door opened a foot or so and Norwood gave his guitar a little trick spin and dropped into a boxing stance. "Whuddaya say, tush hog," he said. But it wasn't Joe William at all. It was a short, bushy-headed young man in a green sweater. He was eating a sandwich. He said, "What is all this?"

Norwood said, "Oh. I thought Joe William Reese lived here."

"Well, he did, but he's gone now. You just missed him."

"Where did he go?"

"Back home. Some place in Arkansas. He left a couple of days ago. You a friend of his?"

"We was in the service together. How Company,

Third Batt, Fifth Marines. He owes me some money."

"I take it you're from Arkansas too."

"Naw, I'm from Ralph, Texas. We used to live in Arkansas but when I was in the seventh grade we moved over to Ralph. It's just the other side of Texarkana. Bowie County."

"I see. Well, how is everything in Bowie County?"

"Just fine. What did he go back home for?"

"Well, as I get it, he was following this girl."

"What girl?"

"Some girl from his home town. I forget her name. She was up at Columbia more or less killing time and she wanted to go to Paris or Italy or someplace but her father said she'd have to put in some time at home first. Reese is trying to marry her. It was all very complicated. I can't remember the details. I gather her family has some money."

"Yeah, I know about her. He's been sweet on her for a long time."

"So. That's the story. He left."

"What was he doing here?"

"Working at the post office."

"He could of done that at home."

"That's true enough. But then the girl was up here. Look, you want some coffee or something? You look pretty beat. I was just having lunch."

"I don't care if I do."

"Come on in."

"I wouldn't mind having a sandwich either."

"Sure thing. I'm afraid all I have is potted meat."

"That'll be fine."

"It'll have to be on hamburger buns too, I'm out of bread."

"That'll be fine."

"This stuff is cheap but it's very nutritious." He picked up the can and read from it. "Listen to this: 'beef tripe, beef hearts, beef, pork, salt, vinegar, flavoring, sugar and sodium nitrite.' Do you know what tripe is?"

"It's the gut part."

"That's what I thought. I suspected it was something like that."

"It's all meat. Meat is meat. Have you ever eat any squirrel brains?"

"No, how are they?"

"About like calf brains. They're not bad if you don't think about it. The bad part is cracking them little skulls open. One thing I won't eat is hog's head cheese. My sister Vernell, you can turn her loose with a spoon and she'll eat a pound of it before she gets up. Some people call it souse."

"Why do they call it that?"

"I don't know. You got to have a name for everything."

"Yes, I hadn't thought of that. Well, they're both good names. *Tripe. Souse.*"

It was a railroad apartment with peeling pink walls and a bathtub in the kitchen. There were two open suitcases on the living room couch and a big pasteboard Tide carton in the center of the room which was overflowing with books and wads of newspaper. A middling big roach was trying to climb out of the bathtub on the lower slope. He seemed addled and he kept slipping back. Norwood sat at the kitchen table and cleared away ashtrays and magazines to make an eating space on the tablecloth. He picked up an aerosol insect bomb and gave a couple of test sprays from it.

"This was where Joe William lived?"

"Yes."

"I figured he'd have a nicer place than this."

The bushy-headed young man was putting a pan of water on the stove. "It's not much, is it?" he said. "But it's not as nasty as the one just overhead, if you can believe that. That was mine. I moved down here yesterday afternoon. The rent's the same. This one is a little more convenient too."

"How much is the rent?"

"Sixty a month."

"Damn. You could make payments on a right nice house for that. Everything is high in New York, ain't it?" He made himself a sandwich and started in on it.

"Yes, I suppose it is. By the way, my name is Dave Heineman."

Norwood shook his hand. "Glad to meet you, Dave. Mine is Norwood Pratt. What are you, an Italian?"

"No, I'm a New York Jew."

"Oh."

"Do you know any Jews?"

"I don't know. I don't think so. Well, there's Mr. Haddad at Haddad's store in Ralph. *We Clothe the Entire Family*. That's what he has on his window."

"He sounds Syrian to me."

"He might be. I wouldn't know the difference. I was in boot camp with a Jew from Chicago name Silver. I didn't know he was one till somebody told me. Instead of saying 'Turn out the light' he would say 'Lock the light.' You couldn't break him from it."

"Why did you think 'Heineman' was Italian?"

"You just look kind of Italian."

"This Silver, was he a pretty good soldier?"

"Well, he wasn't a soldier, he was a Marine. Yeah, he was all right. Except for saying lock the light. What do you do, Dave, do you work at the post office too? Everybody I've met so far works there."

"No, I don't really work anywhere. Here at home. I'm a free-lance travel writer. Just from handouts though, I don't travel anywhere, yet. Sunny and gracious old Lima, city of contrasts, where the old meets the new. Old guys making pots and plying similar ancient trades in the shadow of modern skyscrapers. That's what I write."

"Is there any money in it?"

"Not the way I do it. There is if you can grind it out. What I'm after is trips, freebies, some of that big time freeloading. Once you get on that circuit you're in. My problem is I'm lazy. I've got a Provence piece due at the *Trib* this afternoon and I haven't written a word. I've been sitting here all morning drinking coffee and smoking and reading match covers. Hunt's fabulous tomato sauce recipes. *Draw Me. Finish High School at Home.* Did you finish high school, Tex?"

"Naw."

"I didn't think so. Here, take these, look into that course."

"Thanks. The water's boiling."

Heineman made the instant coffee in two big red striped Woolworth mugs. "How was the trip up?" he said. "Maybe I can do a piece about it. 'See America First.'"

"It was all right," said Norwood. "Some hobo got my boots on the train. He was one more slick customer. He took 'em right off my feet and I didn't see him or hear him. Yeah, and I wisht I could get aholt of that sapsucker. He'd *think* boots. I wouldn't care if it was the hobo king. It may of been the hobo king. He was plenty slick. Well, I'm not being serious there."

"About what, the king?"

"They have got a king. That's right, this is no lie, I read this. They have got them a king just like England and France and he rules over every tramp in America just like a . . . *king.*"

"I noticed your shoes. Your Congress gaiters."

Norwood shifted gears from the hobo realm and looked at his shoes with a puzzled frown, as though he wasn't sure how they got on his feet. "I just picked these things up," he said. "A man give 'em to me. They're not too much really."

"I don't see anything wrong with them. What's wrong with them?"

Norwood twisted one around on his foot. "I do have to say this: They're comfortable dudes."

"Let me get this straight. You're saying that *comfort* and not *style* is the most important feature of that shoe, is that it?"

Norwood was spreading some more meat paste on a bun. He stopped and held the knife upright on the table in his fist and looked around. He looked like an overgrown nursery rhyme character with expectations of a pudding. "Where's the mannaze?" he said.

"There's not any," said Heineman. "You'll have to use that mustard, what's left of it."

"Mannaze is better with potted meat." He scraped the mustard jar with his knife and got the stuff out in little dobs. "How about pickles?"

"No, it seems I'm out of everything, Tex. I didn't know you were coming or I would have laid in some things. Some pearl onions. A relish tray. Perhaps a salad."

"You know, I feel like a fool coming up here all this way and then Joe William is gone back home. I could of stopped off by his house on the way up. I come within just a few miles of it. I didn't even think about that. His folks said he was up here."

"How much does he owe you? If that's not too personal."

"Seventy dollars."

"Yeah, well, I'd call that a fool's errand all right. Even if you had caught him here you probably wouldn't have gotten the money. He's a bigger sponge than I am. He fooled me with that country boy act and got out of here owing me twenty-five."

"How did he go home, with that girl?"

"I don't know if he went *bodily* home with her or not. I think he flew."

"Flew? And here I am riding freight trains and he's the one that owes me money."

"Well, it's not enough to get upset about it, is it?"

"What do you mean?"

"I mean seventy dollars is not really worth all the trouble, is it? Traveling what? Two thousand miles? And losing your boots? Figure it out."

"I was coming up here anyway. He owes me the money. It's not a gambling debt, it's out of my pocket."

"Yeah, but it's only seventy dollars. And what are your chances of getting it back with a guy like Reese? Didn't you ever lose any money before? Hell, forget it. Go on back to—where do you work, Tex?"

"I did work at the Nipper station in Ralph."

"Then forget it and go on back to the Nipper station in Ralph. I think you've got too much anxiety invested in that debt."

"I said I *did* work there. I don't work there any more. I'm a Country and Western singer now."

"All right, the point is, the money's gone."

"I'll get it."

"Okay, have it your way

"Besides, I'd like to see him."

"Okay."

"It's not just the money."

"Okay, all right. It's none of my business anyway."

Heineman got up and went to the refrigerator and

brought back a little carton of cottage cheese. "You want some of this?"

Norwood said, "I don't eat that stuff."

"Good. There's not enough to split anyway." He put salt and pepper on it and ate it from the carton.

"Do you know any beatnik girls?" said Norwood.

Heineman ate and thought about it for a minute. "I know some who *look* like beatniks. I guess it's the same thing. There's one on the third floor. Yes, Marie's a beatnik by any definition. Would you like to meet her?"

"Well, yeah."

"She sings, you know. I think you'll like Marie." He stopped eating and sniffed. He made a face and went to the living room window and leaned out. "Okay, Raimundo, knock off the grabass," he said. "I told you not to burn any more of those stink bombs out there."

Raimundo was the one with the big sunglasses. He and the others kicked up sparks. "It's a campfire!" he said.

"No, it's not a campfire, it's a mattress fire on East Eleventh Street and it stinks. Now put some water on it."

Raimundo went into another defiant spark dance. "We don't want to."

"I said put it out."

"We're having fun."

"That may be, but I don't want you to have any fun. Fire Commissioner Cavanagh doesn't want you to have any fun either. He was on the radio about this very thing. I think I'll call him."

"You don't have a phone."

"Come on now, don't be a pest. It's a neighborhood disgrace. The *Post* will be down here taking squalor pictures."

"I want my fifty cents," said Raimundo.

"Don't start in on that again. You'll get your money."

"When?"

"Soon." He pulled both windows down and came back to the kitchen and resumed work on the cottage cheese. "Little bastards. I hope they all get respiratory diseases this winter."

"If it was me," said Norwood, "I would be ashamed of myself borrowing money from little boys."

"I don't actually borrow it from them. They don't have any to speak of. Raimundo runs a few errands for me."

"Say, is it okay if I shave here?"

"Yeah, that's it right there, the kitchen sink. The john itself is in the back. When you get through we'll go up and see if Marie is in and take her over to Stanley's. I don't feel like doing that piece anyway."

Marie was agreeable in many ways, if a little odd. Through deafness or inattention she never heard anything the first time. *"What?"* she would say. *"What's that?"* She took Norwood up to The Cloisters and twice for rides on the Staten Island Ferry, always wearing the same loose orange silky blouse. She didn't work anywhere and she didn't seem to have any friends. She didn't do anything. Once on the boat Norwood put his arm around her waist and she removed it and said he took a lot for granted and that she would let him know when she was ready to be "pawed." He tried it again the next day but she still wasn't ready. They played guitar duets in her apartment, with Norwood plunking chords, and they sang folk songs from a book.

"You don't really like folk songs, do you?" she said.

"They're all right," he said. "I like modern love numbers better."

Marie was a speech major from Northwestern and one night she read aloud from her favorite book, which was something called *The Prophet,* and Norwood listened and clipped his fingernails. She fed him and seemed to welcome his company but nothing ever got off the ground in the way of funny business. Every night he traipsed back downstairs and slept on Heineman's couch. It was rough and nubbly and left red waffle marks on his face and hands. It was too short too. On the fourth day he got up and toppled on the floor. His legs were dead from the knees down. When circulation was restored he went upstairs and told Marie he was leaving. She said, "What?" and he said, "I said I got to go."

"Oh. You're leaving."

"Yeah, I got to get on down the road."

"Oh. Well. You'll have to write me a long letter about Shreveport."

"Yeah, I'll have to do that."

"About the program and all."

"Okay."

"Well. All the best, Norwood."

"Yeah, you take it easy, I'll see you sometime."

HE WALKED to Union Square in a light drizzle and stopped at the Automat for a dish of baked beans with a hot dog on top. It was the best thing he had found to eat in New York and by far the cheapest. The place was packed with damp bums who smelled like rancid towels and he had to wait for a seat. One fell vacant and he darted in and got it. Then he saw that he had forgotten his silverware. He left the dish of beans on top of an *Argosy* magazine to stake a table claim and went back to the cutlery stand. While he was gone the girl with the dirty dishes wagon picked up his beans and an Oriental gentleman across the table got the magazine. A man with a bowl of oatmeal got the seat. Norwood came back and thought at first he had the wrong table, then he recognized the Chinese gent. He grabbed the magazine from the foreigner's clever hands and turned to the oatmeal man. "You got my seat." The man's fast reply was "I don't see your name on it." Norwood stood there with his knife and fork and paper napkin.

Just then a big man in a blue suit, not a bum but some sort of manager, appeared in the middle of the room and started clapping his hands. "It's not raining out there now," he said. "Everybody who's not eating —*outside!*" He clapped and bellowed and there was a sullen, shuffling movement toward the door. He spotted an immobile Norwood. "That goes for you too!"

Norwood said, "I had some beans here a minute ago. You can ask anybody at this table. Except this one. He got my seat."

"It's not raining out there now. Let's go!"

"I ain't studying that rain, man. I'm trying to tell you that somebody got my chow that I paid good money for."

"Don't give me a hard time. *Outside!*"

One of the bums who was being stampeded called back from the revolving door, "Hey, it *is* raining out here!"

Norwood put his heavy duty silverware down on the table and left. Within two hours he had said goodbye to the hateful town and was speeding south in a big Trailways cruiser. He was thinking about purple hull peas sprinkled down with pepper sauce.

There was nothing to see along the featureless

turnpike to Washington except elbows in the passing cars below. He read his magazine. He dozed awhile. A famous athlete in the seat behind him, now reduced to traveling by motor coach, said, "Niggers have taken over all the sports except swimming. They don't know how to swim."

In Washington there was a layover and a change of buses and a new driver. He was a cheerful fatso with his hat tipped back and although the signs said DO NOT TALK TO OPERATOR he started right in cracking jokes and carrying on with the passengers. Norwood wanted to get in on it and he went up front to scout for a seat but they were all taken. Maybe later. He had two seats to himself at the back. He took off his guitar and put his feet up in the seat, sitting crossways.

Darkness fell and a low white moon was running along with the bus just behind the tops of the scraggly Virginia pines. Norwood had his head wedged in against the seat and the window, using his hat. He watched the moon and made it go up and down by closing one eye and then the other. *Moonlight in the pines . . . and you were so fine . . .* How did people write songs anyway? . . . *Moonlight in the pines . . . and in this heart of mine . . . you were so fine . . . your lips were sweet as wine . . . moonlight on the road . . . moonlight on the*

*bus . . . moonlight on the trail. . . . A Republic
Picture. . . . Hey, Gabby, the widder was looking
for you. Aw tarnation, Roy. Roy and Dale and the
Sons of the Pioneers having a good laugh on Gabby.
Roy's real name was Leonard Slye. . . .*

The bus slowed and pulled over and stopped on
the shoulder. A girl with a flashlight and a shopping
bag full of clothes and a blue and white overnight
case got on, talking away and stumbling on the cord
from some unseen appliance in the bag. She would
have fallen had not the driver, the fat and courteous
J. T. Spears, jumped from his seat to catch her.

"You didn't have to run so hard, little lady," he
said, "I saw you coming."

She was out of breath. "I thought I had plenty of
time. I got to talking there on the porch and then I
saw your yellow lights come over the hill and I just
took off aflying. They were all laughing and hollering
at me, *'Run, Rita Lee, run,'* and then that cord from
my hair drier came aloose . . ."

She was a pretty little girl with short black hair
and bangs and bejeweled harlequin glasses. A little
thin in the leg but not too thin. She was wearing a
bright yellow dress with a white daisy on one side of
the skirt part.

Norwood stood up in a kind of crouch and tried to
indicate that he was friendly and that he had a good

place to sit back there. She came down the aisle and stopped and he stowed her gear in the overhead rack and she thanked him and took the seat in front of him, next to a woman with blue hair.

They hit it off fine, the girl Rita Lee and the woman, and began at once to exchange confidences. The woman was a dental assistant from Richmond with a twenty-year pin who had been to Washington to see how laws are made. It was her first visit to Congress. "People who live right around something don't care anything about it," she said. "I bet if I lived at the Grand Canyon I wouldn't go out and look at it much. And other people would be driving thousands of miles to see it." Her husband had disappeared two years before and was subsequently found working as an able seaman on a sulfur boat, through a rude postcard he had foolishly sent her from Algiers, Louisiana. He was now back home, but living in the garage and drinking.

The girl Rita Lee had been visiting her grandmother and certain cousins in Virginia. She was from near Swainsboro, Georgia. She was now on her way to Jacksonville, North Carolina, for a showdown with someone named Wayne at Camp Lejeune. Although she did not have a ring—she had not pressed him on that—they had had an understanding for more than a year now and she wanted to know what was up. There had been no letter for almost two months.

"What is he, a officer?" said the woman.

"Boy, that's a good one," said Rita Lee. "Lord no, he's a Pfc down there in the Second Marines."

Norwood stuck his head up in the notch between the two seats. "Do you mean the Second *Marines* or Second Marine *Division?*" he said.

They looked up at him.

"When you say *Marines* that means regiment. If you mean *division* you have to say *division*. Now he could be in the Second Marines, Second Marine Division, I'm not saying that. But he might be in the Sixth or Eighth Marines too and still be in the Second Division, that's all I'm saying."

"I don't know what it is right offhand," said Rita Lee. "I'd have to look on a envelope. All I know is he drives a tank down there in the Second Marine something."

"There's nothing wrong with tanks," said Norwood. "Gunny Crankshaw used to be in tanks. That dude had a Silver Star. He shot down the gates of Seoul University. He had all his khakis cut down real tight and he would just strut around like a little banty rooster. Ever once in a while he would stop and take his handkerchief out and knock the dust off his shoes."

There was a heavy silence. The bus swerved to

avoid a big tire fragment in the road but bumped across it anyway.

"That's where somebody throwed a recap," said Norwood. "They get hot enough and they'll just peel right off. You can't tell about a recap. But if I'm driving on gravel a lot I'd rather have one. They'll hold up better. It's harder rubber."

"I think we've had about enough out of you," said the dental assistant. "You're butting into a private conversation."

"I was just trying to be friendly."

"Well, you'll have to get back in your own seat. We can't talk with your head up there like that."

At the bus station in Richmond Rita Lee had a Pepsi-Cola and a sack of peanuts. Norwood moved in on the stool beside her and ordered coffee.

"Whuddaya say."

"Oh, you, hi. Say, I like your hat." She poured the peanuts into the bottle and shook it and fizzed a little into her mouth from an inch or two away. The goobers boiled up in carbonated turmoil. "My hair is just a mess."

"It don't look like a mess to me."

"I washed it and rolled it up and had it looking so nice and now look at it. It was running for that bus. What are you doing with that cowboy hat on?"

"I thought you liked it."

"I'll say this, it's a tall one."

Norwood stirred his coffee and talked to her with his head turned just slightly; he knew he wouldn't be able to talk straight if he looked directly into her face. *What a honey!* It might even knock him off the seat. "This ain't a bad looking bus station for Richmond," he said. "You'd be surprised how little that one is in New York."

"I know a girl that went to New York and got a suckruhturrial job right off making ninety-five dollars a week. She was the FHA Charm Queen two years running. *And smart?* She didn't know what a B was."

"They put butter on ham sandwiches up there," he said. He put a dime in the remote jukebox unit and played a Webb Pierce selection.

"I know why you're wearing that hat. You're a singer yourself."

"How did you know?"

"I saw your guitar on the bus."

"I fool around with it some." He looked in all his pockets and then forgot what he was looking for.

"Have you made any records?"

"Well, I'm just getting started. I may cut some platters when I get to Shreveport." *Cut some platters?*

"I bet you'll be a big star one of these days and

your folks will be so proud of you."

He wound his watch.

"Is that your home, Shreveport?"

"Naw, my home is Ralph, Texas, down there the other side of Texarkana. It ain't too far from Shreveport."

"Have you got a wife anywhere?"

"Naw."

"I was supposed to been married last March. It was all my fault, I said no we better wait. Wayne, see, he wants to do everything right now and after he thinks about it he don't want to do it any more."

"That's a mighty nice dress you got on."

"Thank you, I made it myself. He may have him some old girl down there. That handsome devil, all the girls wanted him back home but they couldn't get him from me. He would favor Rory Calhoun a lot if his neck was filled out more."

Norwood was doing a pushup from the stool.

"What's wrong with you?" she said.

"Nothing."

"You keep doing things."

Nothing was said about it but there was a tacit understanding that they would sit together when they got back on the bus. Norwood did not try anything right away, although much of his discomfort had passed. There in the half-light of the bus he could not see her face clearly. Her voice alone and presence did not stun and confound his brain.

They talked. He edged closer to her through a series of leg crossings and body adjustments. Soon he had his arm over her shoulder. No resistance. He let it slide down a little and began squeezing the soft flesh of her upper arm. It was wonderful. The way he was doing it, with just a thumb and finger, giving a thick pinch here and there, was like a witch testing a captured child for plumpness. Rita Lee couldn't decide whether she liked it or not. She had been grabbed and wrenched about in many different ways but this was a new one. She stiffened.

"I was afraid of this," she said. "I was afraid the minute I sat down here you would think I was looking for love on a bus."

Norwood didn't stop, nor did he answer, not liking to have attention called to what he was doing when he was at this kind of thing. He nuzzled her. "I mean it now," she said, but not with any firmness, and he cleared his throat and kissed her and she relaxed, Wayne the Marine out of mind. He went back to the arm business, still not saying anything or acknowledging in any way that anything was going on.

After a time she said, "Norwood?"

"What?"

"Tell me something."

"What?"

"What is your all-time Kitty Wells favorite?"

"I'd have to think about it."

"Mine is 'Makin' Believe.'"

"Yeah, that's mine too."

"Listen."

"What?"

"I'd like to hear you sing sometime."

"Okay."

"Why don't you sing something now? I'd like to hear something now."

"Not on the bus."

"You could do it soft."

"Naw, not on the bus."

"What is your singing style like?"

"I don't know."

"Yes you do. Who do you sing like?"

"Have you ever heard Lefty Frizzell sing 'I Love You a Thousand Ways'?"

"No, I never even heard of Lefty Frizzell."

"I don't guess I can explain it then."

"You got a scar back here on your neck. It looks awful. There's not any hair growing on it."

"I fell off a water truck in Korea."

"Did you do any fighting over there?"

"I got in on the tail end of it."

"Did you kill anybody?"

"Just two that I know of."

"How did you do it?"

"I shot 'em."

"I mean but how?"

"Well, with a light machine gun. They were out there in front of the barb war and one of 'em hit a trip flare. It was right in front of my bunker and they just froze. My gun was already laid on 'em, except I had to traverse a little and I cranked off about thirty rounds and dropped 'em right there."

"Did they scream?"

"If they did I didn't hear 'em. A bunch of mortars come in and when that let up me and a old boy from South Carolina name Tims went out there and throwed a plank acrost the war and brought their bodies back."

"I bet you got a medal."

"For that? Naw. The skipper didn't even like it much. He wanted a prisoner. He thought I should of run out there with my .45 and said 'You two gooks are under arrest.'"

"You should of got a medal."

"You don't get medals for things like that. Unless you're a officer. They give 'em to each other."

"If I had killed anybody I don't think I could sleep at night."

"That's what we was there for."

"I know that but still."

"It didn't bother me none. It wasn't no more than shooting squirrels. Naw, it wasn't as much because squirrels are not trying to kill *you*. With big one-twenty mortars."

"I never even seen anybody dead close up and I don't want to either."

"Them two needed killing anyway. If they had dropped down flat when that flare went off I couldn't of depressed my gun down far enough to hit 'em."

"Come on now, hon, and sit up a minute. I'm about to fall off this seat."

Norwood sat up and moved over to his side and lighted a cigarette. Rita Lee didn't exactly want this, a total disengagement, and she snuggled up against him and put his arm, dead weight, across her shoulders.

"You're a lot heftier than Wayne is," she said. "He's tall and stringy. His best friend in the Marines is a nigger. What it is, he likes nigger music and nigger jokes. He can talk like one pretty good. After he got his car him and Otis Webb robbed every Coke machine in the county. People commenced rolling 'em inside at night. Otis had to go to reform school because he was sixteen and a nigger and the judge told Wayne he could either go to the pen or the Marines. Wayne took me out to eat at Otis's house one time and their floor was as clean as any shirt you got in your drawer. You're not even listening to me."

"Yes I am."

"Let me have a drag off that."

"This Wayne don't sound like much to me."

"Well, he's sorry in a lot of ways, I never said he wasn't, but he's got a kind heart. I'll say this, the world would be a better place to live and work in if everybody was as nice to niggers as Wayne."

"I guess you got your mind set on marrying him."

"I don't know if I do or not and that's the gospel truth. I don't know if I'm coming or going, my heart is so mixed up."

"What do you aim to do if he don't want to get married?"

"Well, I thought some about going and stay with my sister in Augusta and get in beautician school. She teaches at Mr. Lonnie's School of Hair Design. But she's so funny about people staying with her. She gets to where she sulls up and won't talk and slams doors. It's pure d. meanness is what is it. She needs somebody to just slap the snot out of her."

"You could go with me."

"Go with you and do what?"

"Just go with me. Go to Shreveport with me."

"You mean get *married?*"

"You don't have to get married to go to Shreveport with somebody."

"Boy, that's a good one."

"Well, you don't."

"Rita Lee Chipman does, hon."

"Maybe we'll get married then. When we get to Shreveport."

"You're just saying that."

"Naw I'm not."

"Yes you are."

"Naw I'm not. Really."

"I can't tell if you're serious or not, Norwood. I don't even know you. You meet somebody on a bus and ask them to marry you right off. You must think I'm just a plaything of love."

"Naw I don't."

"You don't even know me."

"I know you well enough."

"What do you like about me?"

"Well. A lot of things. I like the way you look."

"I'll tell you this, I don't like to have tricks played on me. I read a true story the other day about a girl that fell in love with a good looking novelties salesman and he took her to Lewisville, Kentucky, and then run off and left her there at a motel that had a little swimming pool out front. She didn't know a soul in Lewisville, Kentucky. She didn't hardly have a change of clothes. She was just walking around the streets there thinking every minute somebody was gonna jump out and get her."

"Did she go in that pool any?"

"Some woman from the courthouse come and got her and put her in a home. That's where she wrote the story from, it said."

"Well. I told you what I would do."

"I'd have to tell Wayne."

"You could write him a card."

"That wouldn't be right. Either way I'll have to go down there and talk to him."

"You want me to go with you?"

"You better just do what you want to do."

"I'll go down there with you then."

"I was wondering if you would say that."

"Right here is where your novelties salesman would back out."

"Norwood, I think I'm falling in love with you. If you were sick I would look after you and bathe you."

"Yeah, but don't talk so loud."

"I wonder if you really love me. Do you?"

"Yeah."

"Do you think you can say it?"

"I will sometime. Not on the bus."

"You don't mind saying it in a song, why can't you say it talking?"

"A song is different. You're just singing a song there."

"It's not hard for people who really mean it to say it."

"It is if somebody's trying to make you say it. When somebody gets your arm around behind you and wants to make you say 'calf rope,' well, you don't want to say it then."

They reached Jacksonville in the very early morning. The sun was not hot yet but it was bright and painful to their grainy eyes. A dozen or so Marines in limp khaki and with ruined shoeshines were hanging about the station waiting for the last liberty bus back. Fatigue and unhappiness were in their faces, as of young men whose shorts are bunching up. A city cop and an MP sat together in a squad car outside, slumped down in the seat, not talking, and too bored or tired even to go to the trouble of looking mean. Inside the station on a bench some mail-order baby chicks were cheeping away in a perforated box. Bargain chicks. No guarantee of sex, breed or color. Did anybody ever get fifty little roosters? Norwood and Rita Lee passed on through to the café and had an unpleasant breakfast.

Rita Lee was out of sorts. Her cheeks were red from all the nuzzling and she had rubbed them down with some powerful Noxzema. Norwood commented on the smell of that popular medicated cream.

"Maybe if you'd ever shave sometime I wouldn't have to use it," she said.

"I don't have all that stiff a beard."

"What happened to my face then?"

"I don't know. I can use a regular thin Gillette five times."

The waitress was at the end of the counter filling sugar dispensers with a scoop. "Hey Red," she called out, "is yall's sugar thing full?"

"Yeah, it's all right," said Norwood. "We already too sweet as it is anyway." This sally brought a chuckle from the waitress.

"I guess you'd like to take *her* to Shreveport with you," said Rita Lee.

"She don't have enough meat on her bones," he said.

Norwood's idea was to go through channels, to call the reception center at the base or the officer of the day and have this Wayne sent to the proper visiting place at the proper time. That was the way to go about it. Rita Lee didn't like the idea in that it alerted Wayne and gave him time to hide or flee. Her plan was simply to go out there and personally track him down and suddenly appear at this side. Norwood could not convince her that this was unrealistic thinking.

Yes, but that was the way she wanted to do it. And furthermore she didn't want him going out there with her now. Three exclamation marks appeared over Norwood's head. No, her mind was made up. He could wait on her here in town if he was of a mind to. She would be back whenever she got back.

"What time?" he said.

"How do I know? Why? You figuring on leaving?"

"Naw. I just wondered. So I could be here."

"I don't know how long I'll be."

"You ought to be back by dinnertime, don't you think?"

"I can't say because I don't know."

"Well, I'll be here looking for you about one."

"I wonder if you will be."

"Yeah, well I know I'll be here. You worry about your own self being here."

When the shuttle bus backed out of the dock Norwood waved bye to her with one finger. She looked at him but she didn't wave. He watched the bus until it was gone. She wouldn't be back and he had lost a day and $4.65 getting his ticket changed. *Take care of him and bathe him!* He would wait until one but no longer. Catch the first bus out.

He walked about town, down the long main street, but nothing much seemed to be open. The penny arcade was buttoned up tight. A long-armed Negro boy was squeegeeing the windows at Woolworth's, where they were having a Harvest of Values sale. The bargains were spilling out of a big gold foil cornucopia, and were artistically mixed in with one short ton of candy corn. Norwood's eye was attracted to the X-tra soft finespun cotton T-shirts with reinforced necks, three for $1.29.

"Will them T-shirts hold up?"

"Says whut?" said the squeegee boy.

"Them T-shirts you got on a special there, will they draw up on you after you wash 'em?"

"Uhruh, they'll all draw up some."

"That ain't a bad price. I might be back and get me a half a dozen of them dudes. I'm always out of T-shirts."

"You know you right? Man can't have too many of 'em."

Down the street a piece Norwood stopped at a hardware store, thinking he would go in and run his hand through the turnip seed and look at the knives and see how much shotgun shells cost in North Carolina. He shook the door but it was locked. So was the furniture store next door. There was a white card behind the door glass here with a phone number on it and it said call R. T. Baker in case of emergency. *Hello, Baker? I hate to bother you at home but I need a chair right now*. There was a tattoo parlor and

Norwood looked at the dusty samples in the window. He had a $32.50 black panther rampant on his left shoulder, teeth bared and making little red claw marks on his arm. He had never been happy with it. Not because it was a tattoo and you couldn't get it off—so what?—but because it was not a good panther. Something about the eyes, they were not fully open, and the big jungle cat seemed to be yawning instead of snarling. Norwood complained at the time and the tattoo man in San Diego said it wouldn't look that way after it had scabbed over and healed. Once in Korea he sat down with some matches and a pin and tried to fix the eyes but only made them worse. Many times he wished he had gotten a small globe and anchor with a serpentine banner under it saying *U.S. Marines—First to Fight*. To have more than one tattoo was foolishness.

It got hotter and white town soon ran into nigger town. Norwood heard movement in one of the beer joints and he tried the door and it opened. A Negro woman was standing on a chair in there painting the wall dusty pink with a roller. "We closed, hat man," she said.

"Yeah?"

"It's off limits for you anyhow."

"It ain't nothing off limits for me. I ain't even in the service."

131

"Let in all civilians, Ernestine," said a funny quacking voice. "All save one."

Norwood was already inside. A big window fan was blowing hot air across the room. The woman got down from the chair grumbling and went to the door and made a fuss getting it latched. "You the last one coming in till I get that wall Kem-Toned, I don't care who it is. You better not be over the hill either."

The man with the funny voice was a midget of inestimable age. He was sitting on the end of the bowling machine runway with his legs crossed. On his face there was a Sydney Greenstreet look of weary petulance. He was wearing a seersucker suit, an untied black bow tie and some black and white wingtip shoes. "Do go on with your work, Lily," he said. "I'll keep tabs on this young man." He seemed to be drunk, or at least tight.

Norwood got a can of beer from the green cooler, which was an old Dr. Pepper box with a chunk of ice in it and some rusty cold water that made his hand hurt. *Do Not Set On Drink Box* said a handwritten sign that was taped to the side. Another one on the wall behind the counter, a bought one, said, IF YOU CAN GET CREDIT AT THE POST OFFICE YOU CAN GET CREDIT HERE. Norwood leaned on the box and drank his beer. It was good and cold.

"Are you staring at me, you lout?" said the midget.

Norwood turned away from him and watched the paint being rolled on.

"It's very rude, you know. No, you probably don't know. . . . Tell me, what is your I.Q.? It would interest me to know that figure. Do you even know? No, that's a foolish question."

Norwood turned back to him. "My service GCT was a hundred and twenty-five, shorty. All you got to have to get in OCS is a hundred and twenty. I thought it was a right good score myself."

"Ah, a rise. Now I demand to know your name."

"Yeah, well I'd like to know yours first."

"I see. So that's the way it is. I don't suppose you've ever heard of Edmund B. Ratner, the world's smallest perfect man?"

"I can't say I have, naw."

"That's a pity." He shook his can. "Look here, this is quite empty. Be a sport and fetch me one of those tall Buds. My foot is asleep."

Norwood looked at him for a moment, then got a beer out of the cooler and took it to him. "You're too kind," said the little man. "Sit down, sit down. Here's to your wonderful country." He took a long pull from the can. Norwood sat at a table. The man pooched his belly out and slapped it with both hands. It was a sizable paunch. "Disgusting, isn't it," he said. "I told you a lie a minute ago. I am not actually the world's

smallest perfect man. Not any more. I *do* have reason
to believe I am the world's smallest perfect *fat* man."

"Well, my GCT ain't a hundred and twenty-five
either."

"That's very good. You're a better sort than I took
you for."

"You not from around here, are you?"

"Good heavens no. I'm in show biz."

"I figured you must be with some circus."

"Yes, funny little chaps cavorting under the big
top. Do you think all midgets work for circuses?"

"I figured *you* did."

"It's true enough, I did. I worked for all the best
ones too. The Cirque d'Hiver, the Moscow State Circus, Ringling Brothers. All the rest are rubbish. But
the truth of the matter is, my friend, I am now on the
way down."

"I'm trying to get in show business myself. Hill-
billy music. You probably don't like it."

"On the contrary, I do. Some of it. Hank what's his
name—?"

"Hank Williams?"

"No."

"Hank Thompson?"

"No."

"Hank Locklin?"

"No."

"Hank Snow?"

"That's it, Hank Snow. . . . *'cause I got a pretty mama in Tennessee and I'm movin' on, I'll soon be gone.* . . . I once lived in a trailer with a geek, a man of heroic depravity, who played that record over and over. He couldn't hear it enough. He was a nasty drunk, a hopeless sort of fellow, always falling asleep with a cigarette and burning his blankets. Well, they wanted burning, I daresay, but I couldn't put up with that. Live with a firebug? It was out of the question. An absolute human wreck."

"Hank Snow's from Canada. The Singing Ranger."

"What, are you booked in some club here?"

"I never even been on a stage yet. I'm trying to get started."

"Oh, you'll make it. Stick with it. A matter of time, that's all."

"I hope so."

"No doubt about it. It's really quite funny in a way, our paths crossing like this. You're on the way up and I'm on the way down. Two curves on a graph intersecting at . . . this place. Well, that's a bit fanciful. I know I've had too much. But I'm not one of your garrulous, sentimental drunks, so you needn't worry on that score. Dramatizing themselves, as if anyone else cared. No, I've been on my own since I was a child. My father sold me when I was just a pup."

"Sold you?"

"Yes."

"I don't believe that."

"It's true, yes. He sold me to a man named Curly Hill. Those were *dreadful* times! My father, Solomon Ratner, was not an uneducated man but he was only a junior railway clerk and there were so many mouths to feed. And imagine, a midget in the house! Well, Curly came to town with his animal show—he toured all the fairs. He saw me at the station and asked me how I would like to wear a cowboy suit and ride an Irish wolfhound. He had a chimp named Bob doing it at the time. I directed him to my father and they came to terms. I never learned the price though I expect it was around twenty pounds, perhaps more. Now understand, I don't brood on it. Curly was like a second father to me, a very decent, humorous man. He came from good people. His mother was the oldest practical nurse in the United Kingdom. I saw her once, she looked like a mummy, poor thing. The pound was worth five dollars at that time."

"Are you with a circus here?"

"No, no, I thought I told you, I left circus work. Now that was a silly business. I let my appetite run away with me. I can't account for it, it came and it went. Pizzas, thick pastramis, chili dogs—nothing was too gross and I simply could *not* get enough.

Some gland acting up. I grew four inches and gained almost two stone. Well, the upshot was, they took away my billing as World's Smallest Perfect Man and gave it to a little goon who calls himself Bumblebee Billy. I ask you! Bumblebee Billy! All his fingers are like toes. Needless to say, I was furious and I said some regrettable things to the boss. The long and short is, I was sacked altogether."

"Them are regular little hands you got."

"Of course they are."

"If you were out somewhere without anything else around, like a desert, and I was to start walking towards you I would walk right into you because I would think you were further off than what you were."

"I've never heard it put quite that way. Well, it's a matter of scale. I'm not a dwarf, you know."

"Maybe you don't like to talk about it."

"No, it's all right, I'm not the least bit sensitive. I do dislike the way newspapers throw the word around. 'Governor So-and-so is a moral midget.' That annoys me."

"What are you doing now?"

"What indeed. A good question. I would have to say nothing. I lived in New York for the past two years. Opening supermarkets, you know, with second-rate film cowboys. I was an Easter bunny for Macy's and a leprechaun in the St. Patrick's Day parade. That sort of thing. *Terrible!* I thought I had touched bottom. Then last month my agent persuaded me to join a U.S.O. troupe as stooge for this perfectly impossible comedian. You never heard such embarrassing blue jokes in your life. He has little pig eyes that glitter and burn with malice. Just an impossible man to work for. After last night's performance at the Marine post here we were driving back to town and whenever he would say anything I would answer, 'Yes, Mr. Pig Eyes' or 'No, Mr. Pig Eyes' or 'Is that so, Mr. Pig Eyes?' He slapped my face—he didn't hit me with his fist—he slapped me and I gave notice immediately and wired my agent for train fare to the Coast. I'm hopeful of getting some television work."

"You been here drinking all night?"

"Well, no, not here. In my room at the hotel. I was up there drinking gin and 7up and pacing about and trying to read a paperback book but I was much too upset to keep my mind on it. When the gin was gone I came out for some air and that colored lady there, Lily, God bless her, was kind enough to let me in. I'm still waiting for the money order."

They drank some more beer and ate boiled eggs and pickles. Edmund showed Norwood some clippings, a couple of them in laminated plastic, and some photographs. There was a picture of him and the beloved Curly surrounded by dogs, and one of him and a midget woman, both in fur hats, standing in front of the Kremlin. "I hated Russia," he said. "Such a dreary place! I'm bound to say though, in all fairness, that midgets are exempt from taxes there. Don't ask me why. One of Stalin's whims, I suppose." He also had a deck of miniature cards and he demonstrated a royal shuffle. Norwood told him about his trip and his plans and about waiting for Rita Lee.

"I guess that sounds pretty dumb to you."

"Not at all," said Edmund. "It rather depends on the girl, doesn't it? Do you love her?"

"Well, yeah."

"Then there's nothing more to be said. I take the simple view. You must marry her. Everyone should be married, and particularly in a vast and lonely country like this. I say that because I was once married myself."

"If she shows up."

"We had three lovely years together. She was Lithuanian, a fair girl, a little Baltic pearl. She was mad for sour cream. It all fell apart as things will, but still we had the three years. Such memories! She left me for my good friend, Laszlo the Cyclist. At least I thought he was my friend. It was very shabby treatment they gave me. Laszlo pretended to an interest in dominoes—that's my game—and it gave him access to our quarters, and opportunities. The thin end of the wedge. Perhaps I was to blame, I don't know. I have my moods. Well, afterward he came to me and said, 'I hope you are not angry.' There's cheek for you! I said, 'No, Laszlo, I am not angry, but I *am* hurt. You might have said something, you know. We can no longer be friends.' I was very sharp with him."

There was a barbecue shack across the street and Norwood wanted to get some spareribs but Edmund insisted on going back to the hotel because he was anxious to find out about the money. Also, he said, his "seat" was in the hotel dining room. He retied his bow tie without a mirror, put on a tan porkpie straw hat with colorful band, and they sauntered down the street in the noonday sun, this curious pair, Norwood throttling back on his normal pace.

The money had arrived. The desk clerk at the hotel gave Edmund the notice and said he would have to pick up the money itself at the Western Union office.

"Very good," said Edmund. "But I think Norwood and I shall have our lunch first. Can you recommend anything?"

"The meat loaf is all right."

"Splendid."

Edmund had dietetic pear salad and onion soup with croutons and the meat loaf and fried eggplant and blackberry cobbler with whipped cream. He sat up high on his padded riser. It was the kind of seat used to elevate small boys in barber chairs, except that Edmund's was a customized, collapsible model. Norwood had a DeLuxe Cheeseburger. The food was good and they ate without talking. From time to time there was laughter from an adjoining room where the local Lions were listening to a speech.

Shortly, out of a thoughtful silence, Norwood said, "What's the most you ever made as a midget?"

"Net or take-home?"

"That first."

"Two seventy-five a week."

"*Damn.*"

"I thought it would last forever."

"That's a lot of money a week."

"I didn't save a dime."

"How was that meat loaf?"

"Very good. It wasn't jugged hare at Rule's but it was very good. The cobbler was excellent. You're not taking the train, are you?"

"The bus."

"How far west?"

"Well, to Memphis first."

"Do you know if the bus is a Vista-Dome?"

"I imagine it'll just be a regular bus."

"Well, see here, I don't know how to put this, exactly. I'm just a bit apprehensive about traveling cross-country in the States alone. It's silly, I know. Civilized country and all that. But you see, I once had a bad experience in Orange, New Jersey. I was all alone. It could have happened anywhere, of course. Mischievous boys, that's all. One of those things. What I'm driving at is this: Would you and your girl friend mind terribly if I sort of tagged along with you? That is, as far as Memphis?"

"Yeah, be glad to have you. The only thing is, I don't know when we'll be leaving. I might have to go out there to the base after her."

"It's an awful intrusion, I know. Still, I thought, better for you to be inconvenienced than me in a state of terror. I won't get in the way. Trust me on that. I realize three's a crowd."

"Well, not on a bus it ain't, so much."

"This is very good of you. I do carry a tear-gas fountain pen but I can't say it gives me much confidence. I just know it will misfire when I need it. And that's the kind of thing that would make a bully even madder."

The man at the Western Union office gave Edmund some trouble because he guessed wrong on the amount of the money order and because the name was spelled *Batner* on the wire. Edmund had asked for two hundred dollars but the agent had seen fit to send only one hundred dollars, along with a message saying NO MORE ADVANCES FAT MIDGET. SEE FARBER COASTWARD. MILT. Edmund went into a theatrical fury and slapped various cards and credentials down on the counter, which is to say up on the counter. The suspicious clerk examined them one by one, affecting to read all the print on them. It was clear that he disapproved of people whose affairs were so mismanaged they had to have money wired to them.

"Look here, sir," said Edmund, "consider the probabilities. Do you think it very likely that there are two fat midgets in this wretched backwater expecting money orders from New York, one named Edmund B. *Rat*ner and the other Edmund B. *Bat*ner? *Really!*"

"We have to be careful, bud. You run into some mighty funny things in this business."

"Nothing quite that funny, surely."

"If I make a mistake it's my ass, not yours."

"You *functionary.*"

The man satisfied himself that he was not being tricked by a cunning gang of midget money-order thieves and he unhappily released the money. Edmund got his bags at the hotel and they started for the bus station. On the way they were diverted into the penny arcade. Norwood looked in some disappointing viewers billed "Cuties on Parade" and "Watch Out! Hot Stuff!" and stamped his name on a

143

metal disc, then threw it away because the metal was
too trashy and light to suit him. They shot at an electric bear with an electric rifle and made him growl.
No one else was in the place except the woman in the
change booth. Just outside the arcade on the sidewalk there was a gaudy, circus-looking cage affair. A
Dominique hen was imprisoned in it. She was wearing a tiny scholar's mortarboard on her head with a
rubber band holding it in place. The sign said:

JOANN THE WONDER HEN
THE COLLEGE EDUCATED CHICKEN

ASK JOANN ANY YES OR NO QUESTION
DEPOSIT NICKEL AND SEE ANSWER BELOW

Joann moved nervously from side to side in her
tight quarters. Her speckled plumage was all ruffled
up around her neck and in other places it looked
damp and sagged. She was hot. There was a crazed
look in her eyes.

"Poor devil," said Edmund. "I know just how she
feels. This is *criminal.*"

Norwood was getting a nickel ready. "I guess you
have to ask her your question out loud."

"Yes, certainly," said Edmund. "And I would pose
it as simply as possible."

144

Norwood stooped over to face the chicken. "Here's my question," he said, then decided not to ask it aloud after all. He inserted the nickel. A light flashed, something buzzed and Joann reached down in the corner and pulled a lanyard with her beak. More buzzing. A white slip of paper emerged from a slit below. The answer was printed on it in dim purple ink. *Charity Endureth All Things*. Norwood studied it, then showed it to Edmund.

"That's hardly a yes or no," he said. "I don't like this kind of thing. They could at least take her out of the sun."

Norwood ran a fingernail across the wire mesh and made affectionate whistling noises at Joann.

Rita Lee was waiting at the station, her face swollen from crying. "I thought you'd gone without me," she said. Norwood started to kiss her, wanted to kiss her, then thought better of it with so many people around and gave her an Indian brave clasp on the shoulder instead. "Wayne is out in the Mediterranean Sea with the Seventh Fleet," she went on, now crying again. "But I didn't care any more. I wanted to go with you all the time. I should of listened to what my heart was telling me last night." She looked up at Norwood through tear-misted eyes and her hands were trembling in the magic and wonder of the moment.

"I think you must mean the *Sixth* Fleet," said Norwood. "The *Seventh* Fleet is out in the Pacific. They don't have anything to do with the *Second* Marine Division."

Edmund was standing off at a discreet distance looking at the books in a revolving rack. Norwood said, "That midget over there, he's going with us as far as Memphis."

Rita Lee looked at him. "You mean *him?*"

"Yeah."

"What for? Who is he?"

"His name is Edmund and he used to work for a circus. His folks sold him. He's going to California now and he's so little he's afraid somebody is liable to go up side his head on the way. You be nice to him."

He took her over for introductions. "A pleasure, I'm sure," said Edmund. "I've heard so many nice things about you."

Rita Lee was wiping her face with a handkerchief. "I hate for you to see me looking like this."

"Oh pooh, you look very sweet if I may say so."

"That's a nice summer suit," she said. "I like your whole outfit. It's very attractive. You look like a little businessman."

"You're altogether too kind."

There was a wait for the bus. Edmund put on his glasses and got out some thick blue notepaper and

shook his fountain pen a couple of times—the regular
one—and wrote letters. Rita Lee and Norwood sat
next to him in the folding seats and held hands,
squeezing now and then, until it became moist and
uncomfortable. She got up and wandered around, to
the ladies' room and the newsstand. Norwood talked
to a man who said water tables were dropping all
over the country. Rita Lee came back with a frozen
Milky Way and some confession magazines and
comic books. She read about a miser duck called
Uncle Scrooge, and his young duck nephews, whose
adventures took place in a city where all the bystand-
ers, the figures on the street, were anthropoid dogs
walking erect. Norwood read about Superman and the
double-breasted-suited Metropolis underworld. It was
a kryptonite story and not a bad one. He went through
the book in no time at all and rolled it up and stuck
it in his hip pocket. "Did you ever see that dude on
television?" he said.

Rita Lee looked up with annoyance from her duck
book. "Who?"

"Superman."

"Yeah and I know what you're going to say, he
killed himself, the one that played Superman."

"It looks all right when you're reading it. I didn't
believe none of it on television."

"You're not supposed to really believe it."

"You're supposed to believe it a little bit. I didn't believe none of it."

When their bus was called Norwood was looking around for a big paper sack, but he couldn't find one. He borrowed Rita Lee's shopping bag and tamped the clothes down in it hard and tight. "You and Edmund take my stuff and get on the bus and get us a seat. I'll be right back." He didn't wait for an answer. He walked quickly down the street to the penny arcade and opened the trap door behind Joann's cage and took her out and put her in the bag. The woman from the change booth came out and said, "What do you think you're doing?"

"I come to get this chicken," he said.

"Oh yeah? What for?"

He draped a smooth nylon slip over Joann's head. "I got to give her a shot."

"Oh yeah?"

He walked quickly back to the station and boarded the bus. The driver punched his ticket without looking twice at the mystery parcel. Norwood made his way back to where Rita Lee was waving and sat down beside her. He put the bag on the floor between his feet and lifted the slip just enough to expose Joann's head. Rita Lee looked on with incomprehension. "It's a Dominecker chicken on my clothes," she said. From across the aisle Edmund was peering over his glasses. "Norwood, how very plucky!"

"I don't want her on my clothes."

"Don't you like chickens?"

"I hate chickens. They have mites. They're filthy dirty nasty things. All they do is mess up the yard."

"This one has had training," said Edmund.

"I don't care nothing about that."

"I like chickens," said Norwood. "You can go in a chicken house at night and they're all sitting there on them poles facing the front like they was riding an elevator."

"Norwood, I don't want that chicken on my clothes. You hear?"

"There's plenty of room over here," said Edmund.

Norwood lifted Joann from the bag and passed her across. Edmund placed her beside him in a sitting position, her feet splayed out in front and her head upright against the back of the seat. It was an extraordinary position for a chicken but Joann was dazed and limp from all the excitement. Rita Lee began to shake out her clothes.

Norwood soon fell asleep, drowsy from the beer and food and movement. Rita Lee and Edmund talked about horror movies and ate their way steadily through the Great Smoky Mountains. At each rest stop the ravenous little man would get off and bring back new supplies of Cokes and corn chips and Nabs crackers.

Just before dark Norwood was roused from his nap by a small boy in wheat jeans who was causing an offensive disturbance. The nature of the disturbance was this: the boy was running up and down the aisle making the sounds of breaking wind by pumping down on a hand cupped under his armpit. Norwood tripped him and jerked him up and shook him and sent him crying to his grandmother.

Rita Lee said, "That was mean, Norwood."

"Well, that kid was out of line."

"You didn't get your nap out and you're cross."

He stretched and looked over at Edmund and Joann.

"I gave her some water from a paper cup," said Edmund. "I broke up some peanuts for her too but she won't eat. I do think she's coming around though."

"Yall get along pretty good," said Norwood. "You ought to take her out to Hollywood with you. Get her in television."

"I expect I'll have my hands full getting myself into television."

"She's plenty smart for a chicken."

"There's no question about it. I'm sure a good

150

agent could get her something. Perhaps some small role in an Erskine Caldwell film."

"Norwood?" said Rita Lee, who was rubbing a finger over the scar on the back of his neck.

"What?"

"I know what kind of ring I want. It doesn't cost a whole lot either. It's one diamond in the middle and two little ones on the sides with things like vines holding 'em on."

"That's what we'll get then."

"You know what would be nice? Listen to this. What we ought to do is get us some Western outfits that would be just alike except mine would be for a girl. You see, they would match. Then when we have a little boy we'll get him one too. Oh yeah, and if it's a girl I want to name her Bonita. I could probably make hers myself. Anyway we'll all be dressed just alike when we go to church and everything."

"I don't like that idea much."

"Why not?"

"I just don't."

"You didn't get your nap out and you're cross."

That night a suicidal owl flew into the windshield but didn't break it and later they saw a house or a barn burning out in an open field. No one seemed to be around it trying to put it out. Still later, seat trouble developed. A sleepy sailor up front sat down on a milkshake left in his seat by a thoughtless child and was forced to look for a dry seat.

Edmund stirred just in time to keep him from sitting on Joann. "I'm sorry," he said, holding his hand over her, "this seat is occupied."

The sailor was a second class bosun's mate with embroidered dragons on his turned-back cuffs and a lot of wrist hair. He looked closer. "That's a chicken," he declared. "You can't save a seat for a chicken. You'll have to put her on the floor, little boy."

Norwood got hold of the sailor's jumper and turned him around. "That ain't a boy, it's a man. You better get you some glasses. Don't sit on that chicken either."

"You think I'm gonna stand up while a chicken sits down? Well, you got another think coming."

"Go find you another seat."

"There ain't any more."

"What happened to the one you had?"

"There's ice cream in it if it's any of your business."

"I might make it some of my business."

"Yeah, well you'll need some help."

"I don't think so."

Rita Lee was frightened. "Norwood didn't get his nap out," she explained to the sailor.

"We'll see what the driver has to say about this," he said.

"Here, there's no need for that," said Edmund. "I can make room for Joann in my seat. Let's not have any more unpleasantness."

Memphis.

Edmund was standing outside the phone booth protesting. "No, really now, I say, it's too much of an imposition—"

"Hush and be still a minute," said Norwood. He sat down in the booth and closed the glass door. Inside on the pebbled, we-defy-you-to-write-on-this wall someone with an icepick had scratched THE USAF IS CRAP in jerky, angular letters. Under that was WE DIE FOR YOU GUYS—AIRMAN, and under that, YEAH IN CAR WRECKS. Norwood got the operator. She said it would be a quarter for three minutes.

The woman who talked fast answered.

"KWOT is the lucky bucks station," she said.

"Hello," said Norwood.

"Is this KWOT?"

"This is Norwood Pratt over in the Memphis bus station."

"Who are you?"

"I want to talk to Joe William Reese."

"He's outside skinning catfish."

153

"Can you get him to the phone?"

"I don't know." She left.

Norwood waited. The operator asked for another quarter. Then another. His ear reddened and got hot and stuck to his head. He shifted the phone to the other side.

Presently, a voice. "Hello, hello, anybody there?"

"Joe William Reese?"

"Yes, speaking."

"This is First Sergeant Brown at Headquarters, Marine Corps. We've been looking over our books up here and it looks like we owe you some money."

"Yeah?" How much?"

"Our books say two thousand and sixty dollars."

"All right, who is this?"

"I told the Commandant you'd probably want to give it to the Navy Relief since you never did give any on payday."

"*Norwood*. Where in the hell are you?"

"I'm over here at Memphis in the bus station."

"What are you doing in Memphis?"

"Nothing. Just passing through. I thought I'd stop by and see you. I been waiting on this phone all day. Some old woman went to get you."

"Oh. Grandmother. She's not supposed to answer the phone. You're just in time. We're having a family fish fry this evening. Do you like frog legs?"

"Not much, naw."

"Well, there's plenty of catfish. You should have been with us last night. We caught a mess of 'em. Two trot lines."

"Did the turtles get your bait?"

"No, they weren't too active last night. I think they were all attending a meeting somewhere. Look, it'll take me about forty-five minutes to get there. You be over in front of the Peabody Hotel. That's right across from where you are."

"Okay. I got a—"

"We might bust a watermelon later, you can't tell. Spit seeds on the girls and make 'em cry."

"Wait a minute. Hold on a minute. I got a couple of people with with me. Is it okay if they come?"

"I don't see why not."

"One of 'em is a girl."

"That's fine. Anybody I know?"

"Naw, it's just a girl. I met her a couple of days ago. We're thinking about getting married when we get home."

"Boy, that was fast work. What did you do, pick her up on a bus?"

"Yeah."

"Well sure, bring her on."

"Is there some special place you're supposed to get a wife?"

155

"No, I guess they're just wherever you find 'em. Buses, drugstores, VFW huts. Don't be so touchy."

"She's good looking. You never seen me with a girl that looked this good before."

"She sounds like a sweetheart, Norwood. Maybe we can get something in the paper about it: *Mr. Pratt Reveals Plans*."

"This othern is a midget."

"I didn't get that."

"I say this othern with me, he's a midget."

"I don't follow. You mean a short guy?"

"Yeah, well he's short all right but he's not *just* short, he's a midget. He used to be in a circus. You know, a midget. His folks sold him."

"But not to you?"

"Naw, *hell*, Joe William. They sold him when he was a boy. He's about forty-eight years old."

"Okay. Whatever you say. Is there anybody else? Any Japanese exchange students?"

"Naw, that's all. Have you got my money?"

"Yes, I have, I've got it. I'm working. I've been meaning to send it to you. I'm checking cotton acreage."

"That's that government job?"

"Yeah."

"They pay straight time, don't they?"

"No, it's by the hour."

"How much?"

"Two dollars. Sixteen bucks a day, no overtime."

"That's not bad."

"Yeah, it's okay. You furnish your own car."

"You get mileage?"

"No."

"Do you have to have a education?"

"No, not really. You have to carry a stick. Killer dogs lope out from under houses when you drive up."

"I got a chicken over here too. I forgot about her. Have you got some place to put her over there?"

"Look, maybe I better charter a bus for your group."

"Don't get smart about it. This ain't a regular chicken. I wouldn't be carrying just a plain chicken around."

"No, I'm sure there's a good reason why you're traveling with a chicken. But I can't think what it is."

"Well, it's too long to explain over the phone. She was in a box in North Carolina answering questions and it was hot in there."

"I see."

"How's the girl?"

"She's fine. I think she's decided I'm about as good as she's going to do."

Mr. Reese cooked the fish in two iron skillets on a

barbecue furnace, which was under a big black walnut tree. The walnuts were scattered underfoot and looked like rotten baseballs. Mr. Reese was a rangy, worried man in khakis. He knew his business with the meal sack and the grease and the fish, never turning them until it was just the right time. He talked to Edmund at length about a staging area he had passed through in Northern Ireland in 1944 and said he had always admired the English for their bulldog qualities.

The front yard was twenty acres or so of Johnson grass with some polled Herefords grazing on it, two of them standing belly deep in a brown, warm-looking pond, for what comfort was in it. Mr. Reese said Johnson grass had a much higher protein value than people thought and that it played an important role in his feeding program. He was uneasy and defensive, and seemed to be afraid that Edmund was secretly amused at his farming methods. By way of changing the subject he said, "I've got eighty paper-shell pecan trees I'd like to show you before dark."

"I'd very much like to see them," said Edmund.

"Of course they're not all that much to look at. They're just trees."

Edmund had bathed and changed and was now wearing white linen slacks and a navy blue blazer, which he kept thumping lint from.

The house was a sprawling 1928 story-and-a-half nature's-bounty farmhouse, done over with Johns-Manville asbestos shingles ("Not One Has Ever Burned."). The front porch was long and wrapped halfway around one side of the house and there were two swings on it. The rich girl Kay sat in one and made room for Norwood but he said he didn't like to sit in a swing and eat. He had never had any meals in a swing but it was something to say. He sat doubled up in a deck chair, hunched forward and holding the paper plate on the floor between his shoes. He cleaned his bones like a cat and made a neat pile of them. He didn't want this girl to think he made a mess when he ate, whatever else she might think. They watched as Joe William made a howling, dusty departure in her Thunderbird.

"He's ruining my tires," she said.

"It ain't helping your bad universal joint none either," said Norwood.

"What's that?"

"It's a thing on the end of the drive shaft. Yours is shot. Can't you hear that clicking? They don't grease them U-joints like they ought to and them little needle bearings just freeze up in there."

"I better get it fixed."

"You'll have to take that whole shaft out. You know where that brace is right there in the middle that

159

holds that carrier bearing study?"

"No, I don't."

"Well, there's two bolts under there that hold that brace to the frame and if you're not careful you'll twist 'em off trying to get 'em out. And right there's where you got trouble."

"In that case I think I'll have someone else do it. I didn't know you were a mechanic."

"Well, I'm just a shade tree mechanic. I can do things like that. I'd be too slow to make a living at it."

"Have a Fig Newton."

"I don't believe I will, thanks. This fish was aplenty. I never was much to eat a cake."

"Joe William owes you some money, doesn't he?"

"Well, he did. He paid me."

"How much was it?"

"Seventy dollars."

"I hope you won't lend him any more."

"You don't have to worry none about that."

"I keep thinking he'll grow up or whatever he needs to do."

"Are you gonna marry him or what?"

"How did that come up?"

"He's a pretty good old boy when you get right down to it."

"I'm not so sure of that."

"A lot of girls would be proud to get him. He had a really good-looking one out in California. She was crazy about him. She had a car too and she'd always fix me up with somebody and we'd go up to the Compton Barn Dance. We had some good times."

"Yeah, that divorcee with the name. I've seen her picture. She has fat arms. Boots or Tuffy or something."

"Teeny."

"I can just see those two together. The blond bombshell and him with his comic patter."

"She looked pretty good to me."

Mrs. Whichcoat filled Rita Lee in on the judge and told her all about the Butterfields. She told about the one who ran up an eleven-hundred-dollar candy bill in Memphis and forced the family to sell a slave to pay it, and about the one who drained the swamps and how he agitated unsuccessfully for a public statue of himself in the square, like the one of Popeye in the Texas spinach capital.

"They all pulled out and went down to Louisiana later, and just made a world of money doing something," she said. "I forget now what it was. They knew how to make money, you have to give them that. How do you like that fish?"

161

"Oh, it's so good," said Rita Lee.

"I bet you never had any that good where you're from."

"No ma'am, I sure didn't."

"It's not as good as some we've had. Is this your first trip to Arkansas, Wilma Jean?"

"Yes ma'am, it is," said Rita Lee. "Except to Virginia it's my first real long trip anywhere. I been in seven states now."

"Dick Powell is from Arkansas."

"He is? I didn't know that. Dick Powell."

"You can *see* seven states from Rock City," said Mr. Reese. "At least that's what all those bumper signs say. You couldn't prove it by me."

Mrs. Whichcoat turned on Edmund. "Did you ever run across a Dr. Butterfield in Wales?"

"No, but then I've never been in Wales, madam. Unless you count Monmouthshire. Curly hated Wales."

"He was a leading practitioner in some well-known city there," she said. "I can't remember which one. Cousin Mattie corresponded with him for quite a long time. Lord, he may be dead now. That was about 1912. The preachers nearly drove us all crazy then talking about the tariff. You don't hear anything about that any more. They're all on integration now."

Mr. Reese wiped his hands on his apron and

searched the skies. He said he would be surprised if they didn't get a shower sometime in the night. "That low started moving in here about four-thirty."

He knew this because he had a thermometer-barometer on the front porch by the door. It was a big tin affair meant to hang on a storefront. There was an orange rooster on it, smiling, so far as a rooster can be made to smile, and crowing about Marvel cigarettes. The Snopesian tackiness of the thing was painful to Mrs. Reese. Mr. Reese took frequent readings and thought about them.

Mrs. Reese did not come outside until the sun was behind the trees because of her skin. She ate some coleslaw and went about being hospitable in her distant way. There were dark pouches under her eyes which an indoor existence and an uncommon amount of sleep did not help much. Things had not worked out well for her. The young planter she thought she was marrying turned out to be a farmer. Her mother got on her nerves. Instead of the gentle Lew Ayres doctor son she had counted on, the Lord had given her a poolroom clown. She claimed descent from the usurper Cromwell and she read a long paper once on her connections at a gathering of Confederate Daughters, all but emptying the ballroom of the Albert Pike Hotel in Little Rock. This was no small feat considering the tolerance level of a group who had sat unprotesting through two days of odes and diaries and recipes for the favorite dishes of General Pat Cleburne. She often managed to leave the impression that she was in Arkansas through some mistake and it was her belief, perhaps true, that only common people had piles.

Edmund and Joe William had to eat the frog legs. No one else would touch them, tasty morsels, although there was a lot of talk about how they were "considered a delicacy" and about how much you would pay for them in a good restaurant. Mrs. Whichcoat sacked up all the fishbones for burning, to keep them from the dogs, and gathered what was left of the corn-bread balls for her laying hens.

Mrs. Reese said, "Do you have any new hens, Mama?"

Mrs. Whichcoat did not answer at once. For some time now people had been closing in on her. She knew how quickly one of these casual openings could land her in a jam. Had she left the gas on again? Was this a new attack on her open range poultry policy? She considered several incriminating possibilities. "No, just the same old ones," she said.

"It's very strange," said Mrs. Reese. "I was looking out the bathroom window while ago and I thought I saw a gray one out there with a hat on."

"That one belongs to Norwood," said Joe William.

"It's a wonder chicken he brought in from North Carolina."

"Oh, it belongs to *these* people," she said. "I wondered. I couldn't imagine."

"That's pretty funny," said Mr. Reese. "A chicken wearing a hat. I never heard of anything like that before. I guess there's a first time for everything though."

Later Norwood and Rita Lee went around back to check on the subject of all this fun. There she was, squatting in the dust alone, shunned by the other chickens. Norwood held her beak down in a mossy skillet under a faucet. After a few dunkings she drank a little. He found some translucent worms on a chinaberry tree and held them in his hand and tried to get her to eat. She didn't want any. He talked to her and told her they were good and compared them to Safeway grapes. "All right, I'm on give 'em to Rita Lee then. She likes 'em."

"Get away from me," said Rita Lee.

He took the mortarboard off Joann's head but she still wouldn't eat.

Rita Lee said, "Have you ever hypnotized a chicken?"

"I never have."

"You can do it."

"How?"

"Let me see her."

"Wait a minute."

"It won't hurt her. They come right on out of it."

She held Joann's chinless head down to the ground and slowly traced a line in the dust in front of her eyes. A few seconds of this and the chicken lay in position, transfixed.

Norwood said, "I'll be a son of a bitch."

He tried it himself and soon they had all eleven of Mrs. Whichcoat's Rhode Island Reds lying about stupefied. He looked at them, then arranged four or five in a single rank and stood in front of them. "Congratulations, men," he said. "Yall keep up the good work. The skipper just come through the squad bay and there was little piles of crap all over the deck."

"You're silly, Norwood, you know that?"

"I think I'm on take her on with us."

"You're going back on your word."

"I know but she don't get along here with them red pullets."

That night it rained. The wind came up and billowed the curtains and the birds stopped their noise and there was one lone rumble of thunder and then rain. Norwood heard people putting windows down. He waited. Water was dripping outside his window on a piece of tin. When things got quiet again he got up and put on his pants and his gaiters and took a penny box of matches from his shirt pocket and went out in the hall. Rita Lee's room was down at the end by the bathroom.

There were unaccountable cold spots in the hall, as in a spring-fed lake. He stood outside the door for a moment and started to knock, then decided no and quietly opened the door. There was a headboard bumping noise and a frantic scrambling movement on the bed table.

"Hey," he said in a half whisper, "it's me."

"Who is it?" said Edmund. "Who's there?"

Norwood struck a match. Edmund was crouched back against the headboard with his fountain pen at his side. He was wearing shorty pajamas of a golden hue.

"Oh. I was looking for Rita Lee."

"Did you think she was in here?"

"Ain't this her room?"

"No, she's across the hall."

"Oh."

"You certainly gave me a fright."

"I didn't mean to wake you up."

"Well, no harm done." He scratched his head vigorously, giving it a sixty-second workout. "I've still got soap in my hair. Their water is extremely hard."

"I didn't notice that."

"Yes, you can taste it. Very high mineral content."

"Well, I'll let you get back to sleep."

"Did you get your money?"

"Yeah, he paid me."

"Well, look here, do you think you could lend me fifty dollars? I'll have it back to you in two weeks. That's a solemn promise, Norwood. You see, I'm going to be in rather a bind. I've been lying here figuring."

"I'd have to have it back."

"Yes, yes, of course. I feel like an absolute rat but I had no one else to turn to."

"When could I get it back?"

"Two weeks, I swear it."

"Okay. Two weeks."

Norwood took five tens from his billfold and laid them on the foot of the bed. Edmund put on his glasses and got his memo book, chattering all the time, and made a to-do about entering the correct address in his memo book.

"No street, just Ralph?"

"Yeah, that's all. We get our mail at the post office."

Edmund wrote down another address, one in Los Angeles, and tore that sheet from the memo book and crawled to the foot of the bed and handed it to Norwood. "You can always get in touch with me through this chap." He picked up the money. "You're a jewel,

Norwood. A veritable precious stone."

Norwood looked at the little torn page. "What will I need to get in touch with you for?"

"Well, you won't, of course. But if you do, there it is."

"Just so I get it back."

"You can count on it. Please trust me on this."

Norwood left and closed the door, the crawling golden vision still in his brain. He crossed the hall and entered Rita Lee's room. "Hey, it's me," he said. She turned on the bed light and turned it off again. He caught only the briefest glimpse of legs and red slip and arms. He struck a match. Now she was under the sheet and had it pulled up under her chin.

"I thought I'd look in on you."

"What for?"

"Well, it was raining. I thought you might be scared."

"I'm not scared of rain. Nobody is."

"There was some lightning too. In here by yourself and everything. I didn't know."

"All I know is I'm about to burn up in this feather bed. You sink right down in it."

"How's your bed?"

"I just got through saying. It's hot."

He struck another match. Outside some night birds had started up again: *ChipOutOfTheWhiteOak* . . .

169

TedFioRito. . . . Whippoorwills. How did two certain birds get together? And then what?

"Norwood, listen hon, somebody is liable to come along."

"Okay."

"Hear? You go on back now."

"I will in a minute."

"No, right now."

"Okay."

"I haven't even got my ring yet."

"Okay."

"Hear?"

"I was laying there in bed thinking about something, Rita Lee."

"What was it?"

"Well, when we get home and get squared away I'm on take you out to dinner. I'm twenty-three years old and I never taken a girl out to dinner in my life except drive-ins. What I mean is supper but they always call it dinner."

"That'll sure be nice. Do you like Mexican food with a lot of hot stuff on it?"

"Yeah."

"I do too. Listen, here's what I'd like to do: I'd like to live in a trailer and play records all night. See, we'd be in there together with our little kitchen and everything. You can fix those things up pretty nice inside."

"I don't know about a trailer."

"I don't think they cost a whole lot. We could get a used one."

"We'll see about it."

Mrs. Reese gave Rita Lee some sheets and towels and other odds and ends and a jumbo black suitcase with straps on the outside, not a new one but serviceable enough. She also gave her a little talk. Joe William got up late and came in the kitchen and Norwood was sitting there at the table by himself drinking coffee with his hat on and whistling "My Filipino Baby."

"Good morning."

"I figured you'd be out checking cotton today."

"No, not on Saturdays. Sometimes half a day. I've got to do a quick recheck on a colored guy this afternoon but it won't take long. Where's the incredible shrinking man?"

"He's gone. He got up real early and your daddy took him to catch the bus."

"Flew the coop, huh? Well, he was a nice little guy."

"Yeah."

"You want some toast?"

"I already ate."

Mrs. Whichcoat came in the back door with an empty wire basket. She hung it up in the pantry and took off her brown garden gloves. "All the hens have stopped laying," she said. "I didn't get one egg." There was a note of despair in her voice but no surprise. It was as though she had warned all along that there would be treachery one day in the hen house. She went in the living room and turned on the television set.

Norwood said, "We got to get on down the road our own selves."

"You're not leaving today?"

"Yeah, we got to get on."

"You might as well stay the weekend now. I thought we'd go over to Memphis tonight."

"I been on the road too long as it is."

"You want some more coffee?"

"Yeah. Have you got a box or something around here I can carry that chicken in?"

"I expect we can find something."

"How much longer does your job last?"

"Another couple of weeks. Maybe three."

"Is it very hard?"

"No, not usually. We're checking plow-ups now. We go out and make sure they've destroyed what they overplanted. They all overplant. I've got a headache with this one colored guy. You can't tell what he's plowed up. He doesn't have it planted in rectangular fields like everyone else, he's got it in trapezoids and ovals with tomatoes and pole beans running all through it so there's no way you can measure it unless you're Dr. Vannevar Bush. He knows I'll get tired pretty soon and say, Yeah it's okay. Well, they screw him on the allotment anyway. I don't blame him."

"That sounds too hard."

"It's not really."

"I wisht I was home right now."

"Are you going direct to Shreveport?"

"Naw, Ralph first. I'll have to leave Rita Lee there at home for a while and go scout it out."

They drove out to a slough and shot at snakes and cypress knees for an hour or so. After lunch they looked through some stuff in the garage and found a long narrow cage suitable for Joann to travel in. It had once served as a humane catch-'em-alive mink trap, and in fact no mink had ever entered it, such was its humanity. Kay came by in her powerful Thunderbird which nobody in town really wanted to insure and they loaded up and drove downtown and parked under the bus stop sign in front of Junior's EAT Café. Kay gave Rita Lee a little gift-wrapped box with a ribbon on it.

She opened it. "Hey, a cigarette lighter. This is really nice. Thanks."

"That's just what they needed, Kay, an onyx table lighter."

"How do you know what they need? Besides, it's a good one. It's butane."

They sat in the car with the doors open and ate ice cream sandwiches. A young carpenter in striped overalls and with nails in his mouth was fixing Junior's sagging front porch with some new yellow two-by-fours. He had brought his kids to work with him and they were in the cab of a pickup. A little girl with sandy hair was hanging out the window backwards and shaking her head from side to side. "Boy, it looks like the world is blowing up," she said. Kay said, "Don't do that, sugar, it'll make you sick." Two stores down, at Kroger's, a teen-age meat cutter came outside and looked around and then rolled his apron up and leaned back against the building with one foot up and smoked a cigarette.

The little sandy-haired girl said, "Hey Daddy, come here."

"I'll be there in a minute."

"Come here now."

"What is it?"

"Randolph wants to peepee."

"Well, you can help him."

"Yeah, but I don't want to, Daddy."

"Aw *hell.*"

The bus came and Norwood and Rita Lee got on with their plunder and Norwood came back up front and stood on the step. Joe William said, "Let me know how you make out down there with Roy Acuff and Hank Williams and all those guys."

"Roy Acuff is in Nashville, Tennessee, and Hank Williams is dead. He's been dead."

"Well, whoever it is. Look, champ, I'm sorry I took so long on the dough."

"That's all right. Yall will have to come see us when we get us a place."

"Yeah, I'd like to. We'll see what happens. I don't know. You can see how it is here, touch and go. Come back when you can stay longer."

"I'll see you sometime, tush hog. You take it easy."

"Okay."

I HE AIR CONDITIONING felt good. Rita Lee got the window seat. She read stories in her love magazines about a lot of whiny girls who couldn't tell the difference between novelties sales-men and Norwoods. *What dopes!* They could expect no more sympathy from Rita Lee, she who had wept bitter tears with them. Along in the back pages of one magazine she ran across an interesting ad. It offered, by mail and on easy terms, a $79.95 wedding set, complete with solitaire diamond engagement ring of unspecified caratage, and two gold bands. *Rush me free booklet of bargains,* said the coupon, *and tell me how high volume sales can mean BIG SAVINGS for me—instead of BIG PROFITS for the jeweler!* The ad showed a man in a Stetson with a jeweler's glass in his eye. He was holding two six-guns and blasting away over his head at some exploding balloons la-beled *High Diamond Prices.* Under the man were the

words *Yes, Grady Fring is bringing them DOWN!*
Rita Lee tore the ad out and put it away. She would
discuss it with Norwood later, at a good time. It was
not the kind of thing to interrupt him with.

She also saw an interesting sight. On a curve not
far from Little Rock a busload of Elks had turned
over. The bus was on its right side in the ditch, the
front wheels still slowly turning, and the Elks were
surfacing one at a time through the escape hatch on
the left side, now topside. One Elk was lying on the
grass, maybe dead, no ball game for him, and others
were limping and hopping about and holding their
heads. Another one, in torn shirt-sleeves, was sitting
on a suitcase on top of the bus. He was not lifting a
finger to help but as each surviving brother Elk stuck
his head up through the hatchway, he gave a long
salute from his compressed-air horn. The big Trailways cruiser began to slow down. When the man saw
this he turned with his noise device and hooted it—
there could be no mistake—at the driver. Norwood
was talking to a man with bulging eyes across the
aisle who had gone broke in Mississippi selling pre-
mium beer for $3.95 a case on credit, and they both
missed it, that hooting part. They did help load the
injured into ambulances. The former tavern keeper
found a silver dollar in the grass and kept it.

In Texarkana that night Norwood called the Nipper station in Ralph and asked Clyde Rainey to go down to the house and tell Vernell he was over here at the bus station and to come pick him up in the Fleetline. Clyde expressed fears about the Fleetline. He said he could send a boy over in the service truck to get him. He would be glad to do it. Norwood said no, that was all right, just tell Vernell to take it easy.

Rita Lee said, "How long will it take?"

"A good hour," said Norwood. He gave Joann some water and them assembled all their gear in a pile against the wall. They sat down to wait. Norwood didn't see Tilmon Fring over by the pinball machines. Tilmon was watching the games with his hands in his pocket. He was wearing the same suit coat and he still had the orange pack of cigarette papers in his hat like a jaunty press card.

Rita Lee said, "What kind of present have you got for your sister?"

Norwood said, "Nothing."

"You ought to get her something, hon. Even a little something. Girls love to get presents."

"I guess I ought to."

Norwood didn't want to leave their baggage unattended but Rita Lee said she didn't think anyone would bother it since there was a chicken with it. Norwood couldn't figure that one out. They left it there unwatched anyway and walked a few blocks and found a drugstore open. He bought a box of chocolate-covered cherries that was on sale. It didn't look like much when he got it in a sack, away from the display, so he bought a small pillow to put with it, a blue shiny one with fringe on it and a picture of the post office standing astride two states, and the words "Greetings From Texarkana, U.S.A., Home of the Red River Arsenal." It too was on sale. He didn't get Bill Bird anything.

Rita Lee said, "What does your sister look like? Does she look anything like you?"

Norwood said, "Some." He showed her a snapshot from his billfold.

Rita Lee studied it. "People with fat faces have to be careful how they fix their hair," she said. "What's she doing in this junkyard?"

"That's where we live."

"Where's the house? I don't see air a house."

"It's off out there to the side. You can just see the corner of the back porch there the other side of where that dog is standing. The yard don't look like that now. I cleaned it up a whole lot."

"He looks like he'd be a good little watchdog. What is his name?"

"It *was* Buster. I don't know what it is now. He just showed up at the station one day and I kept him. I got him vaccinated and put a collar on him and he stayed about a year and then left again. I never could find that scamp."

"Some nigger probably got him. They'll pick up a little house dog."

"Might of. Or got run over."

"Norwood, listen, how long does it take to get married in Texas?"

"I don't know. I don't think very long."

"I mean getting the papers and all that. Everything."

"I know what you mean but I don't know how long it takes. Two or three days, I guess. Vernell got married in Arkansas. She's got her license up over her bed."

"I wisht we'd hurry up and get where we're going. My eyes hurt."

"We'll be there pretty soon."

They were not far from the bus station when Norwood heard someone calling his name. He knew who it was and he foolishly tried to pretend that he didn't hear. Rita Lee stopped and said, "Hey, that's somebody wants you over there." Grady Fring's Invicta was parked across the street on the apron of a darkened service station. The engine was idling but making no more noise than a rat peeing on a sack of cotton. Grady was looking across the top of the car at them. "It's me," he said. "I'd like to have a word with you if I may." Rita Lee said, "Who is that?" Norwood said, "It's a man I know. You go on down to the staton and keep an eye on our stuff. I'll be there in a minute."

Norwood crossed the street. Grady stood there grinning and waiting outside his car with one arm resting on top of the opened door. Norwood had forgotten how tall he was. "Well, you're back," said Grady. He stuck his hand out and Norwood took it and gave it one shake. "I had a momentary impression there that you were trying to dodge me."

"I figured I'd have to see you sometime."

"Yes, indeed. Who's the chippy?"

"The what?"

"The girl, who's the girl?"

"What was that you called her?"

"A chippy. It doesn't mean anything. It just means a sweet little girl."

"I don't think that's what it means."

"You're in a surly mood, Norwood. *Defensive.* It's the voice of fear. I've heard it before."

"What is it you want?"

"Let's start with what happened to my cars."

"Them was stolen cars, Mr. Fring, and you know it."

181

"Where are they?"

"I left 'em in Indiana."

"Where in Indiana?"

"I don't know. Someplace. I don't remember."

"Were the police in any way involved?"

"Naw."

"You just abandoned them."

"Yeah."

"What about Yvonne? I see her hand in this. The coarse Miss Phillips."

"What about her?"

"Where is she? Where did she go?"

"I don't know where she went."

"And where have you been all this time?"

"I went to see somebody."

"Who?"

"None of your business."

"Look, son, don't try to match wits with me. I'd appreciate it if you'd change your tone. All I'm interested in right now is finding out a few facts. You've cost me a great deal of money and considerable worry. You may be in very serious trouble. I want to know the extent of the damage. Don't you think I'm entitled to know that? What's more, I don't like it. I don't like the way you've abused my good faith in this matter."

"I don't see where I'm in any trouble."

"That's only because you're stupid. What did you do with the car papers? The pink slips and the credit card and all that?"

"I left 'em in the car. Cars."

"You're a real dandy."

"Look, starting right now I don't have any more to do with *you* or them cars. I don't have to talk to you any more. Here, here's your watch, *crook*."

"Yessir, you are a dandy," said Grady. He took the watch and dropped it on the concrete without looking at it and stepped on it with the heel of his shoe. "I could have you locked up right here tonight if I wanted to, did you know that?"

"Yeah, what for?"

"Just anything that came to mind. Vagrancy, mopery."

"I don't think you could do that."

"No? Do you believe your house could burn some cold wintry night? What a tragedy that would be. I advise you to curb your tongue, Norwood, and think this thing through and then give me some straight answers. *Now*. We got off on the wrong foot. Let's try it again. We're not communicating and I think I know why. You think the situation is much more desperate than it actually is. True, you owe me the money for the cars but that can be worked out. I can put you on temporarily as night man at the worm ranch. Perhaps later we can—"

"Burn my house? Was that what you said?"

"I didn't say *I*, the Kredit King, would burn it, no. You misunderstood me. These things do happen though, you can't deny it. They strike the rich and poor alike. Well, come to that, I believe they strike the poor more often than the rich because of their necessarily inferior heating systems. The coal oil stove is a treacherous device. Of course the rich stand to lose more in a fire. There's a certain rough justice in the world. Many of your great philosophers have remarked on it."

"You must be crazy."

"Watch it now. You're taking liberties. Don't make things any worse than they are. Don't let your mouth write a check that your ass can't cash, son."

Norwood was trembling. "I'm through talking," he said, and he made a move to go.

Grady slammed the car door and held up one hand like a traffic policeman. "Whoa, I'm not," he said.

"Get out of my way, you big skinny sapsucker!"

Grady didn't move fast enough and Norwood swung and hit him on the temple with a looping right. Grady ran or danced a couple of steps sideways and dropped to one hand and one knee. Norwood was on him like a bobcat. They fell together and the back of Grady's head bounced on the oily concrete and Norwood hit him five or six times full in the face and mouth, then pressed his forearm down on Grady's neck as hard as he could. "What you gonna do now! Come on, tell me what you gonna do now! Come on, you a big talker!"

Norwood heard someone shouting and when he realized it wasn't himself he looked up and saw a woman out there on the sidewalk in the light. "It's a *fight!*" she was saying. "It's a *fight* over here at this Amoco station! Lord, they're killing each other!" Norwood jumped up and she squealed and ran. He licked his knuckles and blew on them and shook his hand. Grady sat up and groaned. Then he got up on his feet very slowly, coughing and spitting. He stood there bent over and holding his throat. His lower lip was fat and split like a hot sausage and blood dripped on his wingtip shoes and his hard-creased trousers. He leaned against the car with one hand and made loud raspy noises breathing in and out.

Two drifter-looking young men, one of them in a Japan jacket, were standing on the sidewalk looking on. Norwood said, "Yall go on about your business. It's all over." They lingered. Norwood raised his voice. "I said shove off." They sauntered away, taking their time about it. Norwood watched Grady drip for a minute. "Them cars don't mean anything to me," he said. "You just leave me alone, you hear? Just stay away from me. Don't come messing around me or my house or anybody over there. Next time I'll bust your head open with a tar tool. I'll kill you. That's all I got to say."

Rita Lee was waiting at the bus station door. "What in the world?" she said.

"It wasn't anything," he said.

"Yes it was too. Who was that?" She looked at the grease marks on his trousers and saw his puffy red hand. "Hey, you been in a fight, Norwood!"

"I used to work for him. He was messing around with me and I told him not to and he just kept on."

"Did you whup him?"

"I guess so. Wasn't much to whup."

"I'll bet you really socked him. I wisht I could of seen it. Did he cuss much?"

"Naw, not much. How about breaking out that Noxzema?"

Tilmon, a quivering crystal strand hanging from one nostril, came over with his hands in his pockets and watched with a demented grin while Rita Lee applied the cream to Norwood's knuckles. "What do you want?" said Norwood. "Wipe your nose."

Rita Lee whispered, "Hon, don't start anything with him, he looks like a molester to me. He may be dangerous. There's one calls my sister on the phone all the time. They can't catch him. They say he has a twisted mind."

Norwood said, "They won't be none of 'em calling you at my house."

At the very last, critical moment Tilmon swooped up and wiped his nose with his sleeve and then wiped his sleeve on his coat. "I saw you when you came in," he said. "I called Grady and told him. Hee-hee. I remembered your hat."

"Your brother is over at that Amoco station," said Norwood. "He wants to see you."

"I saw you with that girl. Grady thought it was that othern and I told him it wasn't. He's a cutter, ain't he?"

"Yeah, he's a cutter and you're a dandy. You go on over there now and see about him."

BILL BIRD said the place for for livestock was in the trunk but Norwood said it was too dusty back there. Bill Bird rode in the back seat with his feet up on Joann's mink cage. Rita Lee fell asleep almost as soon as she got in the car and she slept all the way to Ralph, rod noise and all. Vernell ate her sticky cherry cordials and asked any number of questions about the girl and the chicken. Norwood answered them impatiently. He drove and took it very easy because of the bad rod. Rita Lee was curled up on the front seat with her head in his lap. Everything on the highway passed them, even ratty old pickups with one light. Bill Bird, speaking loudly against the clatter and into a 35 m.p.h. breeze that was pouring through a broken window, said, "I notice he hasn't said anything about the money."

"What about it, bubba?" said Vernell. "Did you get your money?"

"Yeah, I got it."

"Well, I hope he's happy now," said Bill Bird. "All that big to-do."

"What about it, bubba, are you happy that you got your money?"

"You're just like a parrot, Vernell," said Norwood. "Yeah, I'm happy about it. Don't ast silly questions."

"You don't have to bite my head off."

"Well, I'm tard of answering questions tonight. Don't ast me any more until tomorrow."

"When I was in the Canal Zone the Signal Corps boys had a famous parrot," said Bill Bird. "It was their mascot. It was a parrot mascot. They had trained it to speak into a telephone . . ."

Norwood wasn't in the mood for a Panama story and he turned on the radio. It took a while to warm up, what with the dirt dobber nests on the tubes, and Bill Bird was through with his story by the time the volume came up. They listened to XEG, Monterey, Mexico, the rest of the way in, which was the loudest station Norwood could get. "Listen to that, would you," exclaimed Bill Bird. "Now who in the world would want a Lord's Last Supper Vinyl Tablecloth?" Vernell said, "Not me. I think they're tacky." Norwood pulled into the pea gravel driveway with the white rock borders and stopped the car up close to the porch and turned the key off. Home. He stretched. Rita Lee whimpered and complained like a child when he tried to wake her. He carried her inside and put her down on the couch. "She's a cute thing," said Vernell. "I'm surprised you could pick up a girl that cute on the bus." Bill Bird said, "Yes, I wondered about that. I hope there's not anything wrong wth her." Norwood said, "Mine your own business, Bill Bird," and he went back out to the car to get the rest of the stuff.

ABOUT THE AUTHOR

Charles Portis is the author of *Norwood*,
True Grit, *Dog of the South* and *Masters of Atlantis*.
He lives in Little Rock, Arkansas.